The flight landed on the tarmac. A part. Takeoff was comfortable for him. It was the start of something exciting. But the landing was fraught with danger, at least that's what he told himself. He had never read any statistics on the dangers of landing a plane but assumed that this was where most accidents happened.

Slippery runways, wet tyres, a tired pilot, tonnes of weight hitting hard tarmac. That was where Augustine as a detective saw danger. But he wasn't a detective at that point in time. He was a holidaymaker with his partner Christine and their daughter Nightingale.

And he hadn't been a detective for over a month before that point. He had been a patient. Not his favourite role in life. He had been told to recover from the shattered bone in his upper arm as well as rest the artery that was severed in a knife attack by the killer Darcy Bronersky. Signed off from work until the new year, Augustine had decided to take the family to Javea, Costa Blanca, Spain to see his little sister Angelica and her son Tommy.

The plane halted, seatbelts clicked, and the passengers got to their feet. His holiday would begin when he got off the plane, through passport control, collected his cases and was eye to eye with his sister Angelica. She had come down to pick them up from Alicante Airport. She drove a station wagon style car that was big enough for all of them and their cases.

They headed up the coast along the toll road which was quiet. Locals didn't use the toll road because they weren't in the same rush as tourists. Add an extra half an hour and save a few Euros. That was a formula they liked.

As the mountains passed by outside the windows on one side and the sea passed by on the other, Angelica made conversation on everything from the flight to the weather. Christine made more conversation back, Augustine drifting in and out of sleep in the rear seat, where he had chosen to sit with Nightingale.

He listened to the two women who had only met a couple of times before talk as though they had been best friends forever. He loved the way both Christine and Angelica could do this. It was a skill that had always passed him by. Maybe it was a female thing.

His eyes closed, the toll road changed into a smaller, slower local road. He didn't intend to open his eyes again until they reached Javea.

The Mediterranean splashed against the shore.

"Do you know why there are rocks here and there is sand further down the coast?" the man asked.

"Not a clue," the woman answered.

They had turned up for some winter sun. Both worked from home. No, both worked from their mobile phone. So, they could work from anywhere in the world. The urge to 'do Spain' had taken over a couple of weeks prior and they just upped and left. Money wasn't an obstacle.

"Because this is a rocky coastline. The sand isn't natural. It's been added, probably driven in by the truckload. So, the resorts are sandy while the rest of the coastline is rocky."

She nodded. He couldn't see. He was several steps in front of her, marching along the ragged coastline like it was there to be conquered for the first time. She was looking at the flora that was so different to back home in England. Even the greens of the grasses were different to the greens she was used to at home.

As she walked away from the road where they had left the car, she spotted something in the sea, bobbing up and down. At first, she thought it was a buoy, there to warn passing boats of the dangers of the rocks. But it looked much bigger than the buoys at home.

Then as she got closer, the outline of the object became clearer. She screamed. He came running back. She pointed at the body that was floating aimlessly in the sea.

"We need to get help," he said, running back to the road.

He looked at an empty road. In the summer months this would be packed with people making their way to the beaches, car filled with people, inflatables, towels, sun cream and sandals. At that time, he saw nothing.

She joined him.

"What do we do now?" she asked.

"Only one thing for it," he replied. "Phone the police."

"Do we have to?" she responded.

"I don't want to do it any more than you do. But we have to alert them to that body. It's the right thing to do." He took his mobile from his pocket and checked the signal.

"Can't we use a payphone?" she asked.

"And have you seen one of those on your travels?"

He started to dial.

"Wait," she shouted, pointing to a movement in the distance.

They formulated a plan. They would pass the information on to the vehicle they stopped, explaining that they didn't have a phone between them and needed to dash off. And then it would be someone else's problem.

A minute later, he stood in the road and stopped a station wagon.

"Can we help?" Angelica asked as she brought the car to a halt, pressing the electric window as she did.

"We've seen something in the sea. It doesn't look right but it's difficult to see exactly what it is from this far up. Wondered if you'd take a look and give us a second opinion," the man lied. His lips quivered with every word like he was trying too hard to accentuate the pronunciation.

"What do you think it is?" Augustine asked. "What you think it is will probably indicate what it turns out to be in the end. We don't trust our intuition enough."

"Huh," the man said, not wanting to acknowledge the man who was leaning through from the back seat of the car, his head sticking out in between the two women who occupied the front.

"Come on, Gus, let's take a look," Angelica stated, excited to be sharing some of her brother's detective life. She had always been jealous of the excitement her big brother had been up to all his working life while she was a stay-at-home mum.

"I'll stay here and change Nightingale's nappy," Christine spoke, not wanting to become involved at all. Augustine was hovering between two ideas. He was there for a holiday. He was there to get some vital rest and recuperation after a nasty incident and some surgery to repair damage to the nerves and veins in his arm. But he also felt like he had a duty to investigate. It was in his nature. And that nature didn't stop just because he had ventured to another country. Does a lion stop thinking like a lion just because it is put in a zoo?

Augustine looked at Angelica. It was like the times when they were kids, and he had a full pack of sweets. She had already scoffed all of hers. But she still wanted the sugar rush, the fragrant flavours that the sweets would bring to her tongue. She looked at him with her head tilted to one side, fluttering her eyelids and basically pleading with every inch of her body for him to let her have what she wanted. He acceded. He would always be the big brother. She would always be the little sister. He would always want to make her happy.

He got out of the car without a word.

"So, we're going to have a look? You're going to show me how a detective goes about their work?" she asked, bouncing from one foot to the other, back to the child who had wanted Augustine's sweets.

He nodded. A slight nod, one of reluctant confirmation.

She cheered inside but didn't let it see the light of day. She could see that it was getting under Augustine's skin. And if it got too far under his skin then he would walk away.

"Where did you see it?" Augustine asked. The two had their backs turned to the car, whispering something in each other's ears. They turned around as one, in the same way synchronized swimmers do. She pointed towards the edge. Augustine made a mental note of the two of them in case he needed to refer to it later.

The man was six foot tall, pretty much on the dot. His jean shorts had been cut down from longer trousers. rather than manufactured that way. The white trainers were showing much of the terracotta soil that was prevalent in the area. His white t-shirt bore no writing or labels. The face was a man who looked as though he was built for streamlining. His narrow nose and small ears must have made him an efficient swimmer, Augustine concluded. His blue eyes were outlined in a darkness that looked permanent rather than from a lack of sleep. His manner was as though he didn't want to be there.

The woman was half a foot shorter, even with wedged sandals that didn't look like they would last much longer while worn walking. It wasn't what they were designed for. The cork wedges showed pock marks like they had been attacked by woodworm. But the pitted nature of the rocks between the road and the cliffs meant that any shoes would take a battering there. She wore hotpants that were in the same shade of denim as that of her companion. Her shirt was filled with logos, in fact it looked like it was all logo. One of those designer brands that Augustine didn't pay much attention to and couldn't ever make out the exact wording. All he knew for certain was that it began with an 'M.' Her long blonde hair brushed her shoulders as the wind swirled around the four of them. Her blue eyes shone in the sunlight, making her appear more attractive than the rest of her features in isolation would suggest.

They walked to the edge of the cliff, looking down at the water as they walked. Angelica took a sharp intake of breath as she saw what was clearly a body floating in the water. She got closer, scrambling down the grassy banks to see if she could find a way down. Someone had to rescue this person. They might still be saved.

Augustine was having no such doubts. He had seen enough dead bodies to know when someone was beyond salvation. The way the face was under the waterline, the lifelessness of the limbs, the hue of the skin were all giveaway signs that this was a dead body.

Christine looked over at the cliff from the back of the car. She had leaned across the car seat and used the rest of the back seat of the car as a makeshift baby changing station. Nightingale was a dream to change. She didn't wriggle, her poos were always formed and she never once weed when her nappy was off. Christine hoped that potty training would be as easy, although she had some doubts about that.

She watched, listening to the wind swirl across the clifftops. She didn't know what to expect from Spain in December. So far it had been dry with plenty of sunshine. It was only the wind this high up that had given any indication that it wasn't high summer. Well, that plus the fact that the temperatures were much lower than the summer peak.

As she slowly made her way through the process for changing a nappy, she heard a different noise to the wind. Not knowing what it was, Christine took her attention away from Nightingale for a few seconds, still with her hand across her daughter's chest to ensure she didn't roll onto the floor.

Christine saw the dust before she saw the movement. The car disappeared quickly in the direction of Javea. All she could see was the end of the registration plate – GHJ. Nothing else.

4

The sunshine was battling with the wind. At that altitude the wind was winning out. The coldness of the late afternoon was a foreshadow to the night. A lack of clouds meant that the heat would escape and leave the night one for cardigans and jumpers. Little Nightingale would be wrapped up. The lack of rainfall all year round shaped the landscape around them. Not quite a desert, but not a million miles away. The plants that stood up were wind-beaten and scorched. Augustine had seen a television programme about water where the narrator said all plants had the ability to withstand years of no moisture and then just kick back into life again when rainfall finally arrived. This could even be decades later. But they didn't all activate this genetic survival instinct.

The earth was terracotta – the colour of Spain for many. Angelica had got used to the colour. But for the visitors from the North East of England, it was in stark contrast to the soil back at home. They were used to a brownness much deeper and less attractive. On the drive from the airport to where they were stood, Augustine had seen many houses with this material present. On some it was used as a render. On others it was used to make the roof tiles. But almost every property had some of the local soil present. It made it feel like the buildings grew out of the earth rather than being put there by man.

The sea was ever present in this part of Spain. Looking at the country on a map you would easily be forgiven for assuming it was an inland place. The masses of land in the centre of the nation contained cities and a large chunk of the population. But the coast had an attraction that meant people from all over the world flocked to Spain for their holidays. And that meant people took back home with them memories of the sea, the beach, the cliffs. Cliffs like the ones Angelica and Augustine were stood at the top of. Peering down to the blue and white sea below. The sea was crashing against the rocks, causing spray that made its way up the side of their steep faces. Augustine spotted a ledge where several small bushes were growing, presumably on the back of the sea spray that made its way up there.

"Let's call the local police," he said, watching a bird fly above. It was a white sea bird, not too dissimilar to the seagulls on the beach at home, but it felt like a vulture circling the body bobbing around in the sea below.

"That's no fun at all. I thought when you arrived that things might be a little different around here." Angelica replied with a sadness in her voice that Augustine knew was genuine.

"Didn't you have enough excitement back in England?" Augustine asked. They both knew what he was referring to.

"Tommy's dad is a psycho. I wanted to get away from that kind of excitement. But that doesn't mean I'm due a boring life of watching everyone else have their fun. You get to do this every day. All I want is one day of it."

"He has a name, you know."

"He doesn't deserve a name, Augustine. He lost all rights to being called by his name when he hit me the first time. That's when I stopped calling him by his name. I told myself that he could hit me all he liked as long as he left Tommy alone. I kidded myself that was being strong."

"You are strong, sis."

"I'm stronger than I used to be, getting stronger every day. One day I'll be as strong as the almighty Augustine Boyle, detective Augustine Boyle."

"Some days I feel like the defective Augustine Boyle."

"Everyone wants to be you. I've seen you at the police station. I've lived in your shadow all my life. You get the excitement, the fun, the adoration. All I get is a nutter of an ex-husband and the gossip from the mums I met at the antenatal classes."

"So, what are you saying, Angelica?"

"I'm bored."

"And to change this boredom, you want to investigate what happened to that poor woman down there?"

"Yes."

"I was going to ask you to call the police and then we'd leave. But if you want to stay and see where that takes us, I'm game. But when I say that this stops, you have to listen. Do I make myself clear?" Augustine stated with intent.

"Yes."

"Good."

"I'll make the call then," Angelica replied while grabbing

her phone from her pocket. She dialled and the call was answered within a couple of rings. More efficient than we are back home, Augustine thought to himself. She got off the call and smiled.

"My first ever murder investigation," she beamed. Augustine rolled his eyes.

5

"Hola," Angelica said to the detective as he got out of the unmarked police car. The only thing that made it obviously belonging to a member of the local police was the blue light on the dashboard, just like in the American TV shows of Angelica's youth.

"Hola. Ingles?" he asked in reply. She nodded and then motioned towards the car where Augustine, Christine and their baby daughter were sat. Nightingale was sat upright in the baby seat, looking out of the window at a dragonfly that was making its way along the side of the car, looking for shelter from the wind that was still present at the top of the cliffs.

The detective knocked on the window of the car where Augustine was snoozing. He had got up early because he didn't want there to be any chance he missed his plane. Rather than set an alarm and relax, he decided that he would 'just know' when he needed to be up. It wasn't especially early but he could lie in past the eight o'clock deadline for getting up, getting ready and getting out of there. So, he had broken sleep, waking every few hours to check the time even though the darkness told him he wasn't late.

Augustine stirred. Nightingale smiled at the face that appeared the other side of the window. Christine looked away. She wasn't always comfortable with Augustine's career. She wouldn't have dreamed of asking him to give up something that clearly meant so much to him. But she worried herself sick that he would come home hurt or wouldn't come home at all. Recent events confirmed her worries. He had been stabbed in the arm when apprehending a murderer. He needed an emergency operation. Electra had been captured. Ash needed hospital treatment for smoke inhalation. She thought that a few weeks away from work would be a few weeks away from that potential danger that was ever present when they were at home, and he was at work.

Augustine got out of the car and looked the man up and down.

"Javi Jones," he uttered, holding out his hand. Augustine shook it.

"Augustine Boyle. Well, detective Augustine Boyle actually."

"Not here, you're not," Javi Jones replied. His strong handshake wasn't expected as he wasn't a large man. His wiry limbs that looked so tiny at the wrist and ankle bulked out the closer you got to the torso. His biceps were the work of many hours in the gym every week. His lean yet powerful legs the result of running and cycling up the Montgo mountain that dominated the landscape in this part of Costa Blanca. His face was a scruff of hair that seemed to sprout from everywhere. His beard, his moustache, his hairstyle all looked like they were just a series of hairs that grew in every direction. The rest of Javi's features disappeared into the background in comparison. He wore khaki shorts and a sleeveless khaki jacket over a white t-shirt. Augustine guessed his age at late forties. He was probably about right.

"What have you seen," Javi asked with a hint of several accents in there. Augustine assumed Spanish from the location and Welsh from his surname, but he was prepared to be wrong.

"We were stopped by another car. They asked for help. When we looked down, there was a body floating in the ocean."

"The sea."

"What?"

"It's the sea, Augustine Boyle. The Mediterranean, in fact." The Welsh in his accent came out in the vowels. They were sing-song. Augustine remembered this from his PE teachers back in school.

"Shall we take a look? In the Mediterranean?" Augustine asked. He was keen to get back to Angelica's apartment and relax for the rest of the day. Detective Javi Jones didn't seem the type to accept much in the way of help and they couldn't very well fish the body out from where they were stood. Best hand it over and get on with his life.

Javi nodded and held out his hand as if he wanted Augustine to show the way. Angelica followed the pair of them. She was still excited by the prospect of helping solve a murder, even though it hadn't been confirmed the body had ceased to be living because of the actions of someone else.

"So, how long have you been doing this?" Angelica asked, looking at Javi Jones with a smile. Augustine could sense an interest in him that was far more than just the body in the water. But that was just Angelica. He said that she always collected people, making their acquaintance in case she might need them at a later date. It wasn't cynical, just her way.

"I've been doing this for eleven years," detective Jones responded, matching Augustine stride for stride even though he was the shorter man by a good few inches.

"So, you're a bit of an expert?" she asked.

"Yes. Nothing surprises me now."

"Me neither," she responded, trying to gain some traction in the group. She was the only one who wasn't a detective. She was the only one that had never seen a dead body before that day. But in her eyes, that meant that she was the one with the most to prove. Angelica liked that. She wanted to step out of Augustine's shadow. She was sick of family do's where they talked endlessly about their special relative who caught murderers and put his life on the line every day. Nobody ever talked about how well she was bringing up her son. That was nowhere near as interesting as being bashed over the head or stabbed in the arm by a killer.

The two detectives looked at her, walking between them, looking for every inch someone who belonged in their company. Javi Jones had just met her. He didn't have any preconceived ideas about what she might or might not be capable of. Augustine knew not to underestimate her.

They reached the edge of the cliff and looked down. The body had barely moved in the time they had been there. The waves seemed to pass by under the body and continue on their journey. The dead person remained static. Not a word was uttered by any of the three of them. They looked down and then along to the left, almost like they were tied to the same string. The waves and tide had come from that direction. And the only other things in that direction as far as the eye could see were Javea and the Montgo mountain. It followed that the body probably came from that way.

"I'll get the coastguard to go along and get the body from the water. It won't take them long. There's no way of getting it from here," Javi explained.

"Unless you have a very big stick," Augustine added unhelpfully. He wanted to get things done and then get out of there. But he had an uneasy feeling that this wouldn't be the last he heard of this body this trip. He looked along the coastline and saw the same clifftops repeated all along. Craggy rocks, scruffs of vegetation and a sheer drop from the top to the sea. In the UK these cliffs would be surrounded by fences and safety notices. Not here. People lived with the cliffs and the sea all their life here. They didn't need a sign to warn them that it was dangerous – or a barrier to stop them from falling.

The sea was an everyday part of life near the coast in Spain. The fishing, the swimming, the making money from the tourists. People learned to swim about the same time they learned to walk. It was part of life. No need for local indoor heated swimming pools. No need for expensive swimming lessons, instructors, lifeguards. Just go down to the sea and learn. Second nature. Augustine could see why his little sister chose this place to settle down in.

Javi Jones walked along in the direction of the town to see if he could see any other way the body had made it from the safety of the shore to the danger of the waves below. As he walked off, Angelica moved closer to Augustine and whispered in his ear, "Why did you say that?"

"What?"

"The 'big stick' comment?"

"Well. It's true, isn't it?"

"Not really. Nobody has a stick that long. And even if they did, how would it have the strength to pull up a body? It's not like a fishing net. Don't be weird in front of the locals. We found the body – maybe we're suspects. Being weird isn't going to make him suspect us any less, brother."

"I thought being weird might prompt him to tell us to go and get on with our lives."

"Is that what you'd do with a weird suspect back at home?"

"No, actually."

"Well, Spanish police work in pretty much the same way as British police in my limited experience."

"Point taken. Maybe it's the jetlag," Augustine offered by way of an excuse.

"You flew for less than three hours. And we're only an hour further forward in time difference. You don't have jetlag."

But he was tired. He was tired from getting up so early. He was tired of standing at crime scenes. He was tired of having to explain himself to Christine. She wouldn't be very happy when they got back and settled, he already knew that. He wanted it all over. Javi Jones turned on his heels and started to make his way back towards the two of them. Maybe Augustine would get the rest he felt he'd earned.

"I'll need to head back. The coastguard is on the way, I'm told."

"Aren't you going to wait here for the body?" Angelica asked. Her plan was to find out how long. If it wasn't going to be ages, then she wanted to wait. Tommy wasn't finished with the childminder for another hour or so.

"There's been an armed robbery at the Banco BBVA at the Arenal. Pretty nasty stuff; people waving guns around. Shots were fired. People were hurt. I'm pretty much on my own because of that. So, I don't have the time to stand on a clifftop and watch someone else fish a body out of the sea. But feel free to stand and watch if you have nothing better to do."

Angelica was ready to do just that. Augustine wasn't. He put his arm under his sister's armpit and guided her away from the edge of the cliff. She reluctantly walked back to the car with the two men, Augustine still guiding her in case she got the sudden urge to run back to the edge. He felt like her older brother again. He used to do this when they were kids, and he was given the task of rounding her up when they were due to vacate somewhere that Angelica found far too interesting to want to leave behind. She felt like the little girl again, the one that she had struggled to leave behind. She always tried to skip his grasp. When they were younger, he responded by raising his arm to a point where she couldn't wriggle free. Now they were older, she didn't even try.

"Where's the car?" Javi asked as they reached the place where they had first met.

"No idea," Augustine muttered by way of reply, letting go of Angelica. She looked through the window of her car, making faces and waving at Nightingale who responded by blowing bubbles.

"Can we exchange cards?" Javi Jones asked. "I may have some more questions I need to ask you over the next few days when we get some progress with this case."

"Of course," Augustine replied, reaching for one from his wallet. He always carried around ten in there. And this ten never ran out, mainly because he rarely gave them out. It wasn't like he was in the networking business. Most of the people he met were already dead.

Javi Jones jumped into his car, looking every inch the athletic man his appearance suggested. Augustine creaked as he lowered his aching back and throbbing arm into Angelica's car.

"Why do I get the feeling I haven't heard the last of this?" he asked as he sat down.

6

The apartment was dark. The block it sat in was lit up from the outside. The wind that had been everywhere on the clifftop had subsided as they lowered their altitude. Now it was barely a whisper. Augustine fumbled around for light switches in a place he had never visited before. He pressed one on the outside of the door frame and heard the doorbell go. Better wait until he was inside to start pressing any more buttons, he told himself.

Angelica had dropped them off outside the complex with a set of keys before heading to the Mercadona supermarket and then to pick up Tommy. She needed a few bits, asking Christine what she might need before disappearing along a dirt road at the back of the complex and joining a single lane road that ran parallel to the sea. Christine needed nappies. Not wanting to waste most of her baggage allowance weight on nappies, she decided to pack light in that department and then buy what she needed when she arrived. With the right size repeated in her head a hundred times over, Angelica would bring back what was needed. Nappies plus a few beers, some milk and bottled water, maybe a few snacks – she couldn't remember the kind of thing Augustine snacked on specifically but had a good idea that something sweet would hit the spot.

The lights flickered on like the old strip lights in schools back in the 1980's. Augustine smiled at the memories it brought back. He imagined Tony Harper and Ralph Owens fighting in the corner, Paul James throwing things from his desk and Jayne Bloomfield smiling at him. Oh, that smile.

"That's better," he uttered, looking around. The walls were painted in a muted yellow that hinted at the shade on the outside of the building without being an exact match. The room felt typically Spanish. Knowing Angelica's distaste for decorating, it was probable that it looked the same as it did when she moved in. The sofa was a light beige which both matched the curtains and suited the walls. He could image how light and breezy it would be in the midsummer heat. Nightingale was itching to get out of the pushchair, making grunting noises that confirmed this fact.

Christine hadn't said a word to Augustine since he got back into the car on the clifftop. He knew that she was mad with him for getting involved in an investigation when he was supposed to be resting from all of that. She half wished that they had stayed at home where she could control his movements and know what he was up to at all times.

"Ange said that our room is at the end of the corridor," he said to Christine, looking around the corner to his left. In front of him was a kitchen. The darkness of the corridor only showed him an even darker patch in the shape of a door. He searched along the wall for another light switch, tripping over a pair of shoes on the way. He found it. As the light came on, the door became obvious. Augustine wheeled the suitcases along and dropped them inside the room, only glancing at the décor that was reminiscent of the rest of the place. The understated tones made him feel calm and at home. He knew it was his sister's place just by looking at the way it was all set out. The bed had towels stacked on it, the travel cot was already set up ready for Nightingale. She was the perfect host all her life, except for the few years she spent with Tommy's father. He had changed her. She stopped being the Angelica everybody knew and loved. But it was obvious she was a long way along the journey to being herself again. The thought of that made Augustine a happy man.

He wandered back to the living room to see Christine sat on the sofa looking out of the window. Through the downstairs balcony, to the right, she could see the Montgo mountain lit up by the moon, which was itself obvious in the window directly in front of them. Augustine plonked himself down next to her.

"I don't like this, Gus. You're here to rest. And I want complete rest. Plus, you're dragging your sister into this. Doesn't she have enough going on?" Christine enquired, her top lip quivering. She only did this for two reasons. The first was in times of extreme excitement. Augustine had first seen this one on a rollercoaster. The second was in times of deep concern. Unfortunately, Augustine had seen this on their first date and too many times since. He knew which this was.

But before he could reassure her, the door burst open.

"Uncle Augustine!" Tommy shouted so loud that Christine had to put her hands over Nightingale's ears.

"Tommy! How are you, my friend?" Augustine hadn't seen Tommy for far too long. Tommy was a constant feature when Augustine recovered from the brain injury dealt to him by the serial killer Alaaldin Hussein. Angelica took him round every day. Tommy and his uncle would sit and do the crossword, talk about topics Tommy chose and build a bond. At the time, Augustine thought that it was all part of the recovery process and that his sister would be there for him no matter what. Over time, he realised that she was there to get away from Tommy's father, Patrick. It wasn't that she didn't want to see her brother. It was that the force repelling her away from her psycho partner was stronger than the force attracting her to her brother in need.

"What are we going to do this weekend?" Tommy asked.

"I thought you'd be my guide to Javea," Augustine replied.

"Cooooool. I'll take you to the beach, to my favourite place for breakfast, where I saw the dog with three legs and where mummy sits when I'm working hard at school. Oh, and you can see the school too. You can't go inside – that's just for kids. But you can see it from the street."

"That sounds *so* exciting," Augustine responded. But his time with Tommy was done. The young boy had seen his cousin and his interest had turned away from the uncle to her. They all sat and laughed, played and talked about their plans for the holiday. It wasn't long before the excitement of the day had worn them all out. It was an early night for everyone.

7

"Breakfast?" Angelica spoke as she opened the door to the downstairs room Augustine and Christine were staying in.

"Sounds good sis," Augustine replied, being closest to the door. Christine had her back to the pair, just starting to stir. She was an erratic sleeper. Sometimes it all came easily. She would just set her head on the pillow and then wake up ten hours later. At other times she could take hours to get off, having a night of broken sleep before waking up early the next morning. This was one of the former. The sea air, the flights, the early start and the excitement were all factors. The two glasses of red wine were another.

"We're going to Tommy's favourite place for breakfast, mine too. It's along the Arenal, near to the beach. An Austrian café where the waitresses don't speak a word of English. It's one of the places that forces me to practice my Spanish. And it needs as much practice as it can get. Fifteen minutes good for you?"

"Twenty," Christine groaned from the other side of the bed, turning around with a smile on her face that she put on. She was feeling the effects of the red wine. Not a full hangover but something that she needed to shake off, for sure.

"Twenty minutes it is," Angelica replied with a cheeriness that went with the fact she didn't have a drink the night before. It wasn't that she was teetotal or anything like that. But Angelica knew that a few glasses of wine would get her imagination going even more with the body in the sea.

Twenty minutes later they were all set and ready to go. Tommy and Angelica wore matching blue and white hooped tops with blue shorts and sandals with no socks. Christine remarked on how cute they looked as a pair. The truth was that Tommy watched his mother get dressed before going to his room and choosing his own outfit. The upstairs of the duplex penthouse apartment contained two bedrooms and a bathroom. You could get to the open balcony via either of the bedrooms.

Christine, Augustine and Nightingale were nowhere near as matched. Christine was expecting the cold – it was December after all. She wore jeans and a jumper. Nothing too heavy but enough to keep out the cold if it was there. Augustine was going to make the most of wearing shorts and a t-shirt in December. He didn't get the chance to do that at home. But he did have a jumper tied around his waist in case it wasn't as warm as he'd hoped. Nightingale had been dressed in an all-in-one swimsuit that covered her from ankle to neck. She'd probably been given the right balance of protection from the sun if needed and a bit of warmth if needed too.

"Shall we head out?" Angelica asked. The sun was shining through the windows behind her, lighting up the living room with lines of sunlight appearing through the shade of the blind. Augustine went back to the room to collect his sunglasses. And he was ready.

Angelica closed the door behind them and turned the lock. It was one of those doors that locked as soon as soon as it closed. But the extra turns of the key increased the security. Angelica always did it out of habit but felt that the events of the previous day necessitated as much security as was available. Door locked. Check. Tommy's hand in hers. Check. All windows closed before they left. Check. Escorted by a detective. Check.

The walk to the Arenal took longer than it should have because of Tommy's curiosity about everything. Augustine looked forward to the time when Nightingale would be this inquisitive about the world. Tommy asked questions every few paces. He wanted to know how boats floated when they were heavier than water. He wanted to know why Christine was with his uncle. He asked if they were boyfriend and girlfriend before going off on a monologue about the relationships of the other kids in his class at school.

"Manny is the boyfriend of Lucy. Marina and Alex have been boyfriend and girlfriend for years. Roddy loves Martina. But she doesn't love him back," and so on.

Tommy's enthusiasm was infectious. The group smiled and chatted like they had all the time in the world. They pretty much had.

As they arrived at the Austrian café, it was busy. It always was. Finding somewhere to sit could be an issue, especially if you wanted to sit outside. Luckily a group got up from a large table just as they arrived, so they slipped straight into the freshly vacated spot.

Angelica ordered in her best Spanish. Augustine could pick up the odd word, recalled from his Spanish GCSE lessons at school. He was sure whatever his sister had ordered would work for everyone sat at the table. He watched Tommy mouth the words as his mother ordered. It was at that moment Augustine realised that growing up abroad would give his nephew access to another language. He wondered how he could provide Nightingale with that kind of education without moving away from home.

The food arrived in dribs and drabs over the following ten minutes. It was an 'everyone dive in,' meal rather than people being given their own portions. Augustine imagined this was how all Spanish people ate. He didn't bother looking around the other tables in the café to confirm his assumptions.

As the last remnants of food made their way onto Augustine's plate, as they inevitably would, the weather started to do its thing. The early morning cloud had been burned off by the heat of the sun. It was going to be a glorious day. The only clouds in the heavens were those wispy ones that would disappear as they got higher and higher in the sky.

"Well, I think a few hours on the beach are in order," Augustine announced, not knowing at that point that his plans for the morning were just about to be interrupted. Five minutes later his phone rang. He recognized the number as the one for detective Javi Jones from the day before. He had taken the time to key it into his phone, so he knew when the local police were calling him.

"Augustine speaking. Who is this?" he asked even though he knew who it was.

"Augustine, it's Javi. We spoke at the cliffs yesterday. I'd like to ask you a few questions, if that's OK?"

"Fire away, I'm all ears," Augustine replied, turning his body away from the rest of the group.

"Not over the phone, if you don't mind. Could you come over to the police station. It's on Plaza Constitución Española. In the port. I'm sure you'll find it. Go to the desk at the front and ask for me by name."

"OK," Augustine replied. And he clicked off. He knew what it was like to investigate a murder case. He wanted to enjoy his holiday and stay on the good side of Christine. But he couldn't let the man flounder. The family of the victim deserved a resolution. They deserved an answer. They needed someone to drive this investigation forward and find the killer. And Augustine didn't want another body haunting him in his dreams.

"We're going down to the beach when I've paid up," Angelica explained when Augustine turned back to face the rest of them.

"I'll catch you up in half an hour or so," Augustine responded.

"Nope. What do you think you're doing? We're on holiday," Christine pleaded. She knew it would fall on deaf ears, but she had to make her feelings known.

"Half an hour, an hour at the most. I promise."

"You've already doubled it. First half an hour, then an hour. What is it that is more pressing than spending time on the beach with your daughter?" Christine asked.

"The detective has asked me to meet him. He says he has to ask some questions. Christine, I know what it's like to chase a murderer. He needs to make as much progress as he possibly can in the first two to three days. If I can help him then I feel duty bound."

"One hour. And I expect to see you back on the beach in not a second longer. Understood?" Christine asked.

Augustine nodded. Christine walked off with the kids. Then Augustine held out his hand to Angelica for her car keys. He would race back to the apartment and then go to the police station.

"No. No way. I'm going with you."

Augustine didn't want her to follow him into the investigation of a murder. He was used to it. But with the clock ticking on the hour he had been given, he had no time to argue.

They walked back to the apartment saying very little. The excitement had taken over for Angelica. She wanted to see what it was like to chase down a criminal. All Augustine could think about was getting back before the hour had passed. Everything he looked at morphed into an hourglass with the sand running through more quickly than he thought possible.

Angelica moved a few strides ahead of Augustine. She had learned to walk at high speed after having a child and needing to get them off to sleep in first a pram and then a pushchair. Augustine looked down at his sister who was a few inches shorter than him. Her long brown hair looked like it had been drawn from different heads. The multiple shades of brown present made Augustine jealous. His one-tone brown was now sporting flashes of grey but there wasn't the same life in it that Angelica had. Her hair was glossy, bounced as she walked and made her look for every inch like someone in the shampoo adverts. She spent half an hour on it every day, washing, conditioning, drying and styling. But it was half an hour well spent. She wasn't quite as pleased with it. Where he saw condition, she saw split ends. Where he saw beautiful shades, she saw inconsistency.

Angelica didn't go in for much else in the way of a daily routine. She didn't wear makeup, preferring the sunshine to get through to her skin and provide a glow in a more natural way. She wore sunscreen every day because too much of the harmful rays of the sun would take that natural look away as the years passed. Her clothing was relaxed and comfortable. She only dressed up once a week, to visit the other mums in her circle. They were a bitchy crew, moaning their way through life. Angelica didn't get involved with talking others down, but she had known these women since she moved over, and Tommy started playschool. She felt part of the crowd.

Augustine liked the way his sister had turned out. As a child, she was awkward, even what some might call geeky. He sometimes kept his head down when someone asked if they were brother and sister. It wasn't that he disowned her but felt like she was bringing down his street cred. And he needed to protect that as much as he possibly could.

They reached the apartment where her car was parked. A click of the keys and a flash of the lights and they were in. Now to head to the port.

8

The sand on the beach was reassuringly cool. Christine had started to feel the effects of the strong coffee in the Austrian café and the heat of the morning sun. It wasn't especially hot, but she had become so unused to the heat of that yellow orb in the sky that it had taken her by surprise. She estimated the temperature at the high teens. But that was at least fifteen degrees warmer than it was at home.

She took her footwear off and allowed her feet to sink into the sand. She smiled at the feeling. There was something about sand around the Mediterranean that felt different to the sand back at home. She had felt it in the Med and something different again in the Caribbean. The sand on the beach in Javea felt like it had been sieved to ensure it was fine enough to give the twin feelings of softness and granularity. She loved it, not moving for a full minute while the kids she was with had both travelled off in the direction of the sea.

Tommy was following Nightingale as though he was her minder. She crawled slowly towards the sea, but it was still a good two hundred yards away from where she had escaped to. She couldn't crawl that far in twenty minutes, let alone the one-minute head start her mother had given her. Sitting up, Nightingale grabbed a handful of sand and raised it to her mouth. Before she could put the stuff in there, Tommy grabbed her arm and said, "No."

Christine arrived on the scene and smiled at the two cousins playing on the sand in December. She wondered what life might be like if they moved overseas. She always had a soft spot for Australia, visiting relatives there when she was a kid. But it was far too far away from the comforts of home – the people, the food, the lifestyle. She supposed that was the point.

"You guys go and play. I'm going to set up here," Christine spoke to the two children after kneeling down, so she was on their level. It was something she had been shown in a YouTube video on parenting tips. It made sense. The best way to stop kids feeling like they were being talked down to was to remove the physical truth that they were actually being talked down to. "And Nightingale, don't eat sand."

She watched the kids with buckets and spades, boules and a pop-up tent that had all been purloined from the bottom of the pushchair Christine struggled along the beach with. Pushchairs certainly weren't designed to push along the sand, she thought to herself. They should be called pull chairs for this activity. She looked to her left and saw a walkway made from wooden planks along the beach. It was far closer than the promenade. She would head back that way. By then she would have Augustine and Angelica to help her travel across the sand.

The beach was starting to become occupied. The volleyball nets further to her left, beyond the walkway, were attracting attention. An impromptu game had broken out, apparently from different groups of people who had turned up at the same time for the same activity in the same place. It reminded Christine of the football games she saw spring up as she played as a young girl. Jumpers for goalposts, rush goalies and shots from here there and everywhere.

To her right were more people doing exactly what she had –

setting up for a few hours by laying towels on the sand. She had put all of the towels in one square, the five touching each other at the edges. Most others had put their towels out individually. But they weren't one woman and two kids. It was the weekend. The whole family had come out. Around fifty minutes until she was a family unit again, she told herself.

The sea crashed into the shore. The red flags were out. And there were several coastguards on duty. One sat at the top of a tall chair where he could see the whole of this portion of the beach. She looked and saw another ten-foot chair in the distance along the beach. The other two lifeguards in her view were female, dressed in the kind of red swimsuits made famous by *Baywatch*. Christine always fancied herself as a bit of a Pamela Anderson. She had the same red swimsuit for swimming lessons in school. She wanted to get a blonde wig to complete the look. Her parents wouldn't let her.

The kids were throwing sand at each other. Christine resolved to give them thirty seconds to stop, or she would step in. They didn't last more than one face full of sand each, stopping by experience rather than by parental guidance. Christine loved this way of living. Kids heard the word 'no,' far too much in their formative years. Best to let the internal 'no,' deal with it instead.

A couple walked past hand in hand. They were in their twenties and looked like they hadn't a care in the world. Christine felt stuck. It was a large gap since her twenties and felt like a huge chasm until her baby daughter would be in the same age bracket as the two lovers walking past. He had his top off. His muscles rippled as he walked, flexing from the ankle up to the head. She wore a bikini that was clothing only in name. There was so little of it that the fabric it was made from must have been smaller than a handkerchief, Christine mused.

She watched some more, taking in all of the sights of the beach as she relaxed. Well, relaxed as much as she could with a couple of energetic kids playing in and around her feet.

9

"Ange, what the hell is that?" Augustine asked, picking up her phone as it buzzed. He'd picked up a couple of words as the text message displayed on the screen. He really didn't like them.

"I get a few of them. Just ignore them."

"Patty?"

Patrick was Tommy's dad, Angelica's ex. Augustine had the annoying habit of still referring to him as Patty. The abuse he aimed at Angelica caused her to drop the nickname and refer to him by the moniker he was given at birth – Patrick. He didn't like that name. Another good reason to use it as far as she was concerned.

Augustine took his eyes off the road for a few seconds. He was comfortable driving on the right. It didn't seem like an adjustment to him. He just jumped in the driver's seat and got on with it. But, for some reason, he had a little more trouble when he got back home. The transition back to the left was much more of a challenge. He looked at Angelica's reaction. Being in the police for decades gave him an uncanny ability to read reactions. The one he was witnessing was a mixture of upset and casual. The casual was her typical response to this. The upset was because her brother had seen the message too.

"So, you've had more of these?" he asked, already knowing the answer.

"I get them every now and again. This one is especially nasty. But none of them are what you would call nice."

"Well, from the words I saw on the screen, it's vicious. I can't think of another word for it. So, is it Patty?"

"I don't know. It's not the number he had when I left him."

"I guess a sly man like that wouldn't be that stupid. Do you mind reading the whole message out to me?"

Angelica read it out to Augustine. She blushed at some of the personal parts. The message talked about the pain the author would give her when they next met. It referred to inserting something in a place she absolutely wouldn't want anything inserted. It felt totally weird reading it out to her brother - that was for certain.

"Ange, you need to tell the police about this. You can't be in this position again. You have Tommy. And you have nobody else around you in case something happened. Will you report it?"

"Yes, but not now. Maybe you could look into it."

"I'll take a look at all the messages and the number they came from later."

"Numbers."

"Numbers?"

"As in more than one number."

"We need to talk," Augustine uttered in the most condescending way. He meant it to come across like that.

"We're talking right now big brother."

"You know what I mean."

Angelica changed the subject by giving Augustine directions. They were in the port area of Javea, and she knew he was against the clock. It worked. He concentrated on the road. But she also knew that he would come back to this at a later date. She just had to get her game face on, ready for that conversation. It wasn't one she relished with her brother.

10

They pulled up at the local police station. No need to go to reception and ask for Javi Jones. He was there on the steps of the station with a disposable coffee cup in his hand. He was a reasonably short man. Augustine had been told that people were shorter in hot countries because they used up more energy dealing with the heat – leaving less energy to help grow. He had no idea if that was true or not.

Javi had dark hair. If it wasn't black then it was very, very dark brown. It still sprouted from every possible direction. Augustine believed that it had grown in the time since they'd last met. The clothing was the same. Javi always wore the same clothes for work when the weather allowed, which was more than three hundred days a year in the sunny Costa Blanca. He could have just come from a run up the mountain or a bike ride from Moraira or Dénia up and down the coast. But in fact, he'd been hard at work since early that morning. Javi believed in getting as far ahead as possible before most people had even started their daily grind. He imagined that criminals had a lie in. He would be hours ahead by the time they even got out of bed.

"Hola, Javi," Angelica shouted as she got out of the car and waved. Javi responded with a wave and no words. He was a man of little words. The ones he did use counted for something, every time.

"Shall we go inside?" Javi asked.

"Is there somewhere to get a coffee in there?" Angelica asked by way of reply.

"There is. But the coffee is no good, from Portugal. If you want good coffee, then I can show you somewhere."

"Is it far?" Augustine enquired, watching the clock so he could be back to the beach as quickly as possible.

"One minute walk. Thirty seconds walk back," Javi responded with a glint in his eye. His accent looped into the same as the locals every now and again. You and I might refer to it as Spanish. But a true local would be offended by that. They spoke Valencian. And the language of Spain is Castilian, not Spanish. But whatever it was, Javi had the same inflections, the same way of pronouncing each vowel wholly with a depth that English speakers didn't have.

"Why only thirty seconds back?" Angelica asked, knowing that his half-answer was a prompt for one of them to ask that very question.

"It goes right through you."

Sat in a café that looked like it had been converted from a public lavatory, the three of them sipped coffee, exchanging approving glances. The tiles on the floor were a mix of brown and yellow, not in any way flattering. Augustine had seen them in a few places already as they walked along the Arenal and the port areas of Javea. They must have been in plentiful supply at some stage.

"Why have you asked us here?" Augustine enquired, again with one eye on the time. Angelica was looking in the other direction like she was on the edge of the conversation rather than right in the middle of it. She was listening intently, just not participating.

"What exactly did you see?"

"When? At the coast? The body?" Augustine replied.

"Yes."

"We saw a body floating in the water. It was immediately clear that it was something that shouldn't be there. You know, when you see a scene and your subconscious tells you that something isn't right. That's what I got."

"Thank you. Anything else?"

"Just the direction of travel. Obviously, we were there longer than you, so we saw it come from the direction of Javea to south. Do you have the post-mortem results yet?"

"No. We're busy looking for a new coroner. I think there will be one in the next couple of days. The last one quit. And we don't have many murders here, Mr. Boyle. That means we don't have as much need for a coroner as other parts of the country like Madrid or Barcelona. I understand that the chief of police is interviewing potential candidates today and tomorrow. If we don't have someone in place in the next few days, then I'll make an application to have the body taken to Valencia or Alicante. But I'll hold tight with that as long as I can. I'd prefer someone local to do it – someone on our staff."

"What do you think the cause of death is?" Augustine asked, slipping into his usual role.

"I'll ask the questions if you don't mind," Javi retorted. "You couldn't have seen the body from the road."

"No."

"So, how did you know there was a body down there in the sea?"

"We were flagged down on the road by a couple. They asked us to have a look at what they had seen in the Mediterranean. We went closer to have a look, they drove off," Angelica interjected. She was ready to be part of the conversation.

"So, who was it? Who flagged you down?"

"I don't know. They drove off when we got close to the sea," Angelica continued, now standing up facing the two men who were sat on high stools, leaning against a bar that had been decorated with the same brown and yellow tiles as the floor. They must have been really cheap at some stage in the past.

"Descriptions?" Javi fired back. The tension between him and Angelica was high. Augustine was trying to work out whether they already knew each other before the body the day before. Angelica wasn't like this with people unless they got a long way under her skin. Or when she liked one of the boys at school.

"He's tall, narrow face, blue eyes, English. She's five foot five, long blonde hair, blue eyes as well, English as well I'd say."

"Any redeeming features?"

"Not that I can think of. Neither wore glasses, no facial marks, no tattoos on display," Angelica responded.

"Except one," Augustine added. "I spotted a tattoo on the right ankle of the man. It looked like a snake. If I had to guess, then I would say that it wrapped its way around his foot."

"And why would you say that?" Javi enquired.

"Well, what's the point of a snakehead without the rest of the snake?"

"Suppose that makes sense." Javi replied. "Did you get a description of the car?"

"Nothing. We didn't think they would drive off. And we were in a rush to get back home."

"Nothing?"

"It was dark."

"The car?"

"Yes, the car. Can we help with anything else?" Augustine asked, sipping the last of the delicious coffee and getting to his feet. He looked at the clock on the wall of the café and saw that his hour was fast disappearing. Just enough time for a couple more questions and then a drive back to the beach.

"I don't think so," Javi Jones replied.

"We'll be on our way then," Augustine stated.

"Oh, there is one more thing. Almost forgot. We have the name of the person. She is called Maria Valverde."

"Maria?" Angelica uttered slowly, with a tear forming in the corner of each eye.

"Do you know her, sis?"

"She's one of the women who meet up every Saturday afternoon for a chat, sometimes a drink. I've known them since Tommy went to playschool. I need to sit down for a few seconds."

Augustine held her arm and helped her up onto the stool, just to ensure that she was steady and wouldn't fall, he could see that the news had hit her hard. He looked at Javi Jones. The Spanish detective was watching Angelica intently as though he wanted to gauge her reaction to the news. Whatever he thought he might see wasn't present, so he returned his attention to Augustine.

"Please look after her," he said and walked out of the café. His concern wasn't enough for him to stay with the siblings, but Augustine took it as genuine anyway.

"Who is Maria Valverde?" Augustine asked.

"Like I said…"

"No, more than that. Other than that. Who is she?"

"We get together pretty much every Saturday. There's six of us, all mums together; all facing the world together."

"They're a good bunch?"

"They're a bitchy bunch but that bitchiness is usually aimed at people outside of our group."

"Usually?"

"Well, there have been a few arguments of late between

them. Nothing I've been party to, but gossip travels fast."

"And I bet a couple of these arguments included Maria?"

"How did you know, Augustine?"

"I've been doing this for a while now," he replied.

They left the café and headed back to the beach. Little did they know that their day was going to be even more eventful.

The sunshine was blazing down on the beach below. By the time Augustine and Angelica arrived, Christine had retreated to the shade of one of the palm trees with the kids in tow. The three of them were playing sandcastles. That was to say Christine was building them while Tommy and Nightingale were knocking them down. The only dark spot on their play was the fact that Christine couldn't make them quickly enough for the kids liking.

"Hey," she said to the siblings as they approached. Her mood had lightened with the sunshine and sand. It was noticeable to Augustine who responded with a huge smile.

Augustine and Angelica joined forces with Christine, and they built as many sandcastles as they could manage in five minutes. The kids sat down and watched in awe as the sandcastles added up. They were ready to start knocking them down only a minute or so in, but Augustine told then to sit and watch, wait until it was finished. When the grownups were too tired to build any further sandcastles, they let the kids loose on their construction site. The parents sat and talked.

"So, what did the detective want?" Christine asked.

"He told us who the victim was. It's someone I know, Christine. It's one of the mums from the group. She's called Maria. Or at least she was…" Angelica spoke with her voice breaking. She was upset at the fact death was so close to her. And she wondered what would happen to Maria's child. She couldn't imagine Tommy having to deal with something like this. She had moved to Javea because of the peace and quiet, particularly in the off season. But the low crime rate was another factor. There was scarcely a murder there over the previous decade. And now there was one so close to her it hurt.

"Oh, Angelica, I'm so sorry. Are you OK?" Christine asked.

"I don't know what to think. Or what to say. And I'm going over to see the Girls On Tour this afternoon. That's what we're called – Andrea came up with the name. We're from all over the world and came together here in Javea. It's like we're a pop group on a world tour. Now one of us is missing. What do I do?"

"Just be yourself, Angelica. They will need a big arm around them right now. And I can't think of anyone better to deliver that," Christine consoled her.

"Thank you."

"And did he want anything else?"

"Wanted to know how we saw the body from the road. He didn't know that we'd been flagged down by someone else. We never told him that," Angelica replied.

"More like he didn't ask," Augustine added, with his detective's hat on.

"So, does he think they are significant?" Christine enquired, getting lost in the investigation she told Augustine to steer clear from. She chastised herself and took her attention to the kids who were still making their way through the sandcastles.

"He does. And so he should," Augustine responded.

"What did you tell him?" Christine asked.

"I told Javi what they look like."

"So does that mean we're significant?"

"Huh?" the siblings said in unison.

"Well, if he wants to know about them, he will want to know about us. We're just as likely to be involved as the people who stopped us. In fact, as far as the detective is concerned, there is no 'other people.' We have given him descriptions and nothing else. We could have easily just made those descriptions up. How does that make us look?"

"I don't think he'd be sharing as much information as he has with us if he thought we were in some way responsible," Augustine explained. At least that's the way he would conduct an investigation back at home. Surely the way you investigate a murder case crossed international boundaries?

"So, how is he going to find these people that we could have just made up completely?"

"Couldn't even give him a description of their car," Angelica replied with an air of defeatism in her voice.

"I have some of the registration plate. GHJ. That was the last three letters. Will that help?" she asked.

"Well, it's better than nothing, Christine," Augustine replied.

He and Christine sat together and constructed a text message to Javi Jones. It might help, it might not. But it was better than nothing. And Augustine knew that any piece of information in a murder investigation might turn out to be the one that cracks the case.

While they texted, Angelica was concentrating on a text of her own. She had never replied to any of the abusive messages, telling herself that it would just escalate things. But she was drawn towards responding this time. She wanted the person at the other end to know how it made her feel. Maybe that was what they wanted. But she couldn't help herself. Angelica put together a few sentences and hit send without thinking.

She smiled for the first few seconds, looking at the screen on her phone for a reply. It wasn't forthcoming. And then a fear of recriminations came over her. When she thought about just herself, she felt brave. She felt like she could take on anything and she was scared of nothing. But when she thought of Tommy, the text made her sense that she had put him in danger. He had never been mentioned in the messages. But the abusive text messenger clearly knew her.

She returned to the others with a tremble in her voice.

"Tommy and I will be going to see the girls this afternoon. Do you have a key?" she asked before meandering her way back to the car. She didn't want to meet up with the girls. But she was intrigued at what they had to say. Angelica wanted to catch Maria's killer. And she feared the killer might be in her circle of friends.

"Once more into the breach," she muttered.

Tommy looked up at her.

12

Angelica pulled up at the large house in the hills overlooking Javea. The women she hung around with had stacks of cash. She was the only one who arrived in her own car. The others liked a Saturday afternoon drink, and all took a taxi to the house where most of their meetings occurred. Two o'clock, Saturday afternoon. That's when it happened. They met up, chewed the fat and then went their separate ways for a siesta and then to get on with their day. When they first started these meetings four years prior, the kids all needed a great deal of attention. But now they were all older, they would disappear into their own world and let the adults chat.

Driving over, Angelica thought about the events of the last day or so. The body in the sea seemed exciting at the time. She got a little glimpse into Augustine's world. She loved hearing about what he did. But she disliked the way that everyone compared what she did in a negative light. Bringing up Tommy as a wonderful boy and functioning member of society was valuable in its own right. But deep down she did have a desire to do something as exciting as he did. She felt a buzz when they were able to help Javi Jones think about who had put the body in the sea.

The abusive text was the start of the downhill from that buzz. She worried about Tommy. Whatever happened to her, happened. But whatever happened to her also happened to Tommy. She would protect her child with her life. Any parent would do the same. And she was on guard. She didn't think that the killer was linked to her via the texts. But it was one hell of a coincidence. One that made her aware of every movement. She looked in the rear mirror more than usual on the way over to ensure that nobody was following her. She took a different route to the one she normally drove. All of this to give her some peace of mind.

The drinks happened every Saturday. So, why wouldn't they happen this week? She'd not been told by anyone that the Saturday get together had been cancelled. Like Christine said, this is probably the time when they needed each other the most.

The Girls On Tour were generally a good bunch. Yes, there was bitchiness. Yes, this sometimes ended up in arguments between them. But they all had simple desires in life – to enjoy their time on this planet and to have the best for their children. Angelica couldn't argue with those sentiments.

As she walked into the house, the atmosphere was far more subdued than usual. The tequila slammers and loud music of normal weeks had been replaced with glasses of wine and an eerie silence. Angelica would still stick to her cups of tea. She had brought a selection of teabags with her, all fruity. She liked a cup of fruit tea.

She looked around the room. Angelica was going to ask a few questions. She wanted to know if Maria's killer was in her midst.

13

Augustine and Christine, the two -ine's as he liked to call them, sat on the beach with a sandwich each, bought from one of the many choices of a place to eat at the Arenal. She had gone and chosen.

"Get me anything. You know what I like," was his instruction. She chose a ham sandwich. Nothing like the ham you get back in the UK - something more aged, thinner cut and fuller in flavour. Augustine approved.

She had the same. She liked ham. Christine refused to read up on foods that she really liked. In her mind, you could be put off anything. Just looking at the headlines in the newspapers at home when she walked past a newsstand, you could be given cancer or heart disease by pretty much anything. So, she decided some time before that she would avoid the things she didn't like and eat the things she did without the guilt associated. Ignorance was bliss on her palate.

They ate while Nightingale slept in the pushchair. The sea air and all that running around had brought her afternoon nap forward. Her parents hoped that it wouldn't bring her 'wake up' time earlier because they planned a siesta of their own.

Augustine took the time while their mouths were full of food to think about the situation he was in. He was champing at the bit to get involved in the murder investigation. He loved nothing more than catching killers. He felt like that was what he was designed to do. But he was torn between that and spending quality time with his family. He had managed to fit this trip into his normally busy work life because he was signed off from active duty. The injuries sustained in bringing in a killer had sent him to hospital. He wasn't deemed fit enough to carry them out in the UK. Why would he be fit enough to carry them out here?

"Christine, I want to help the detective over here," he said in a quiet voice, one that was designed to keep the calm.

"And I want you to be safe. We need you."

"I know. But I can't rest knowing that the world is a less safe place for Nightingale. When a murderer appears, I feel that I should be part of the world that puts things right for the future generation, especially our daughter."

"I understand. But there are so many murders. You can't solve them all."

"But I can solve the ones I'm close to."

"Agreed," Christine replied. She could see that this was eating the man up. His life had been devoted to catching criminals. And now he has another motivation. He wanted the world to be a better place for their daughter to live in. She could totally understand that sentiment.

"I don't know about you, but I've been looking forward to one Spanish tradition more than any other," Augustine spoke with a glint in his eye.

"What's that?"

"The siesta."

The couple laid down on the bed with Nightingale asleep in

the travel cot at the end of their bed. The sleep came quickly. But for Augustine it was no different to what he experienced at home. He was visited in his dreams by the bodies of the victims he couldn't help. He really didn't want Maria Valverde to join them.

14

Angelica watched the busy nature of the people she had become close to over the previous few years. The group of mums had been meeting regularly for so long that they already knew what each other would do or say in given situations.

But this was completely different.

Nobody knew what the other was thinking. Nobody knew how the other was feeling. They had only the vague notion of grief, knowing that it was a different emotion for each and every other person in the room.

Angelica scanned the bar and saw the couple whose home it was making drinks. It was a large open plan downstairs living area with the kitchen, living room and dining room all merged into one. The whiteness of the room was overwhelming when the sun hit it in the wrong spot. Thankfully that was mainly in the summer. The sun shone that day, but it was much lower in the sky, meaning that the house in front of it blocked a large part of the excessive sunlight. Still enough that they weren't sitting in the dark but not enough that they were all wearing sunglasses and holding their hands over their faces. Angelica had long suggested blinds, but Gerard and Andrea didn't want that.

Gerard had chosen the place, Andrea the décor. He had made millions on the stock markets both as a broker and a speculator. They had a seemingly endless supply of cash. Both wore clothes as white as the room; both with peroxide blond hair. Money meant a great deal to the couple who could have been mistaken as twins. Their height, their mannerisms and their features all looked similar enough to have indicated this.

Gerard's hair was much shorter than Andrea's, but only because he'd recently had it all cut off for charity. He auctioned it off, raising a few hundred Euros for the charity supported by the local mayor – the one which helped look after migrants who had travelled over the Mediterranean in an attempt to get away from the oppression on the other side of the sea.

"Cuppa?" Gerard asked Angelica in his best mock English accent. His Spanish roots were as long as anyone's in the area. He'd paid a researcher to go as far back as possible with his family tree. He was a distant relative of King Ferdinand II, a fact that he repeated to any new acquaintance. He believed the link deserved reverence.

"Aye, go on," she responded, reaching in for a hug and a kiss from both Gerard and Andrea. She knew he was mocking her. His dislike for the English who landed and settled in his country was legendary. He ignored the fact he married an English woman who invited mainly English friends over. Angelica grabbed her collection of teabags and handed them over to Gerard, inviting him to pick one.

"Apple? This is tea?" he asked before pouring boiled water over it and handing the cup to Angelica.

"Yes. Tommy, why don't you go and find the other kids?" she asked. It was more of an instruction than a question. Tommy didn't need asking twice. He was another that Gerard made to feel nervous with his attitude.

Angelica sat on the long white leather sofa that she always

felt was too hot and sticky to sit on in the winter. But it did feel good. The leather was as soft as any she had touched. And the quality of the cushions meant they were a pleasure to sit on – far better than the IKEA cheapo she had at home.

She glanced along to the other end of the sofa and saw the longest, most slender legs in the room, probably that she'd seen in her life. And that could only mean one thing. She was seated with Briana. She had often been called Rihanna with the connection to the pop star. But Briana was most definitely her own name. She hadn't jumped on that bandwagon.

"Hola Angelica," she said, unfolding and refolding those long legs. The tan was all-natural. It didn't fade at any point through the winter. This was for two reasons. The first was genetics. The second was her holiday home in the Caribbean. Briana's long brown hair was straighter than anything Angelica could manage with her own locks. She had asked her friend many times how she managed to get her hair in that ad-perfect condition but never received an answer. Angelica wasn't going to stop asking. Briana was never going to tell.

"Hola, chica. How are you?" Angelica asked. She could see a tear run through the makeup on her friend's face. She shuffled along and gave her a hug that lasted far longer than would normally be comfortable. When they parted not another word was said. Briana's expression indicated that she didn't want to talk. Angelica wasn't going to force things. She just had to see how people were reacting. Briana wiped her eyes with a tissue that had come from somewhere. Her outfit was so small and fitted that Angelica had no idea where she could had secreted even a tissue, let alone anything else. Briana wound her hand around the wine glass that had been sat in front of her the whole time. Her neon pink nail polish glistened with the combination of sunlight and the rosé wine. She looked down at the state of the tissue, took a big swig and then retired to the bathroom to touch up her makeup. She didn't want people to see her as anything less than perfect.

As soon as she raised from the chair, her place was taken by Carmen.

"Move your feet, lose your seat," she uttered as she dropped to the chair and bounced back off again. She had a drink bottle in her hand. Carmen had such a reputation for spilling her drink that she was now given her beverages in a sealed drinks bottle. She could still knock it over, but there wouldn't be the same result of broken glass and the whole drink on the carpet, flooring, rug, sofa or friends.

"How are you taking it all?" Carmen asked in her own inimitable style. She was the life and soul of the party – always the first to arrive and most definitely the last to leave. And Carmen didn't know how to deal with things in any other way than to continue being her normal self.

"I'm OK. How are you?" Angelica responded, studying Carmen's eyes to see how much her friend had drunk.

"Yes, yes. We must celebrate her life, not mourn her death. Isn't that the way we do things around here?"

Carmen had drunk far more than she should. And it wasn't even half past two. Angelica could see her driving Carmen home later, insisting that she hold her head outside the car in case she vomited. Even in her thirties, Carmen had no idea how to handle her drink.

Carmen had been a beauty queen in her youth. She travelled across the country and took part in beauty pageants. As she got older and her childish looks turned to adult, when the beauty pageants stopped, she didn't know how to handle not being told that she was the most beautiful every weekend. She turned to drink. It aged her fast, much faster than the lack of plaudits. Having a child was the last straw for Carmen. She stopped caring what anyone else thought and lived a comfortable life. Among a group of glamorous friends, she wore a tracksuit to these weekly meet ups. The purple tracksuit looked like it hadn't been washed for a while. She wasn't short of cash. Her divorce made sure of that. In fact, she wouldn't have to work again a day in her life, nor would her son if that's what he chose.

"Here's to beautiful Maria," Angelica said, only loud enough for her and Carmen to hear. She still wasn't sure how anyone else would act.

As Briana resurfaced from the bathroom, the rest of the group all congregated in and around the white sofa. There were enough chairs to go round but that last of the group decided she would stand at the back. That was typical Delia. She had to be the one that was doing something different from the rest. She liked to give the impression that she was the strong-willed member of their clan. But when you scratched the surface, she listened to the others and copied what they did. All the strong will in the world didn't give her the imagination to live her own life.

Delia had been named after the British chef Delia Smith by her Spanish mother who had spent a summer in Norfolk after finishing university. She found it difficult to make friends, and the TV cookery shows of Delia Smith were her comfort when she was lonely. By way of thanks, even though the chef would never know, she named her first born after her. Delia Gimenez had never forgiven her mother. She hated the name but didn't have the heart to change it while her mother was still alive.

"Hear, hear. Let's all raise a glass to the life of our wonderful friend, Maria Valverde," Andrea uttered. Glasses were raised, some more quickly than others.

Delia raised hers only after the others had taken theirs back down. She smiled a fake smile, her short dark hair parted at one side, so straight that it could have been drawn in by a ruler. Her hair was always perfect. Her clothing always looked like it had been designed specifically for her. Maybe it had. Her family were one of the richest in the Valencia region. She lived in a mansion along the coast at Gandia when she was young. She hated it. Having a child was the perfect excuse to get out of there and set up on her own. She picked Javea because it was close enough to shout for help but far enough away to ignore her family's shouts for help when they came in the opposite direction. Delia always told herself it was down to the way the wind blew.

"So, how do you think she ended up in the sea? Do you know if she has any enemies?" Carmen asked, getting straight to the point. Drink loosened her lips. And there was no stopping her now.

"She always played her cards close to her chest," Andrea responded. "And what a chest!" she added with a smile. The friends would talk about each other's bodies. Plastic surgery had made it unacceptable to be anything other than happy with every aspect of their bodies. Angelica was thankful she didn't have the money to spend on that. She wouldn't bother even if it was free.

A slight chuckle made its way across the room.

"She was always doing some deal or another. Perhaps one of those has gone wrong?" Carmen said. A glance between Briana and Delia shot across the room like electricity. It happened so fast that if you weren't looking in the right direction, you'd have missed it, But Angelica was looking in the right direction. She stored that one for later.

"I don't know if she was seeing anyone at the moment," Delia asked, changing the subject. Another flash of connection. Another 'blink and you'll miss it' moment. Angelica saw a look from Andrea to Gerard that could have knocked him off his feet. Angelica stored that one for later too. She was glad she was sober.

"I've not seen or heard of her and a man since that guy from the restaurant at the Arenal," Briana added.

"The waiter?" Angelica asked, always behind on the gossip.

"No, the guy who owns the restaurant. The waiter was a onetime thing a few years back. Are you really that far behind the times?" Briana asked. Angelica nodded. She struggled to keep up at times.

"I for one would love to find out who it is," Carmen shouted, still taking large swigs from her drink. She was slurring and the drink spilled around her mouth and onto her chin. She definitely wasn't going to make it much longer at that rate.

"I second that," Angelica responded.

"Yes, me too."

"Hear, hear."

"I want to know too."

The friends stopped in silence after this latest bout of cheerleading. They wanted to raise each other's spirits. But this wasn't the way to do it. People looked out of the window, down to the floor – pretty much anywhere that wasn't at each other. This lasted for a few minutes before the conversation kicked into life again.

"Did you see what the mayoress was wearing at the ball on Tuesday?" Carmen asked the others.

"I know! How much pink can one woman wear at once? She looked like a flamingo on acid," Delia responded.

"A flamingo? I was thinking more of a blancmange!"

The bitchiness had started. Angelica tuned out. She sat back and let it all fly around the room. She had her thoughts on two other things. Firstly, on her friend Maria. And secondly, on who her killer was.

15

Angelica arrived back home earlier than usual. Tommy took ages to drag away from his friends and the gadgets in their rooms. He had a tablet and an Xbox, but nothing like the plethora of tech devices in the rooms of his wealthy friends. Well, if he looked at it in more detail, they were the children of his mum's wealthy friends. But that was splitting hairs. He got on with them all. They accepted him as part of their group.

The excitement of having his uncle Augustine, Christine and Nightingale back at home seemed to be the thing that persuaded him to get ready in half the time it usually took. The journey back was a quiet one. Tommy often chatted away to Angelica on the way home, pestering her to buy the latest game they were playing or the newest piece of kit the others had just been bought by parents who had no idea what these things could do. But that day he had nothing to say. Angelica liked it like that. She had so many thoughts bouncing around in her head that she didn't want him to add any others.

Back at the apartment, they went in and started to get ready. The agreement to go out for something to eat had already been made. Augustine wanted to treat his sister for her hospitality. And there were enough choices within a twenty-minute walk to dine out every day of the year, or so it seemed.

They all got ready, taking it in turns to use the shower so they didn't take water pressure away from each other. Angelica thought it funny that she had the poorest water pressure of her life living this close to the sea. But it was what it was. It was pretty much impossible to have both showers running at the same time. The second one to be turned on would steal the water from the first. All you would be left with was a trickle of cold water that wouldn't even water a houseplant, let alone rinse the shampoo off hair.

They chose the Arenal and then chose Pizzeria Pepa. It was one of the most popular places to eat in Javea, gaining great reviews from locals and tourists alike. Augustine was in the mood for a pizza. He was pretty much always in the mood for a pizza. Christine and Angelica were not. But the pasta dishes there sounded great. They waited for a table and were seated near to the promenade.

People walked past in family groups. Augustine watched people hand in hand, children running forward before dropping back and rejoining their parents. The elderly were treated with a respect that reminded him of the way old people were treated when he was a kid.

Scooters, bikes, roller skates, walkers, runners and people selling goods all mingled in a relatively narrow space without ever bumping into each other. The sea lapped against the shore, only ever giving away its location in the dark through the gentle sound of the crowd. People eat late in Spain. The afternoon siesta is followed by a light snack and then evening activity before having their evening meal. And 'evening meal' is most definitely the phrase that fits. Augustine and Christine were used to people eating at five on the dot back at home. It wasn't a routine they could fit into because of Augustine's work and Nightingale's sleep patterns. But they were aware it was a thing.

'*This is the North. Dinner's at twelve, tea's at five,*' Augustine was chastised with when visiting the home of a suspect once. The man had taken umbrage to the fact Augustine had visited him at teatime. Didn't he know not to interrupt a man's meal?

In Spain, the restaurants didn't open at five. Most were around seven, some later. And this was the time when the places were empty. The locals would be ready for their food a good couple of hours later than this. At quarter to eight, this was as late as they could manage to push their appetites back. Plus, Tommy and Nightingale would be heading to bed pretty soon after. The world passed by. They ordered their food. Everything seemed right. Christine loved the lifestyle she had seen since they arrived. The sea, the sand, the sunshine and the food. And all of this in December when everyone back home had the heating on, and the curtains closed.

"I'm looking forward to my pizza. Extra chillies!" Augustine exclaimed.

"I'm not looking forward to sharing a bed with you," Christine responded.

"Or a toilet with him!" Angelica added.

"I'll be fine. I'm known for my resilience to heat."

"It has to come out somewhere, bro."

As the three of them sat and chatted while Nightingale and Tommy coloured in with books and crayons Angelica had cleverly brought with her, they could see a queue forming at the side of Pizzeria Pepa.

"Good timing on our part," Angelica stated, the others nodding.

The table next to them got up, leaving their payment on the table, stuffed into the menu. A member of the all-male waiting staff grabbed the menu and started to clean up. There were only dessert plates to clear. She had eaten a slice of cheesecake that was covered with fresh fruit. He'd eaten most of the panna cotta he'd ordered.

As the table became free, two people were escorted there by a separate member of the waiting team.

"Hello there," Angelica said as they sat down.

"Gerard, Andrea, this is my brother Augustine, his partner Christine and their daughter Nightingale."

"Pleased to meet you," Andrea stated in the loudest voice. She loved meeting new people and smiled her biggest smile for the relatives of her friends. Gerard nodded in their direction without a smile or a word. But it wasn't as cold as he normally was with new people. He let Andrea break the ice then he would start to warm up himself.

"And we're pleased to meet you," Christine uttered.

"It was Gerard and Andrea's place I went this afternoon. They have the most fabulous house up on the hills. We go there most Saturdays," Angelica explained to the two -ine's.

"You should have come up with Angelica," Andrea said, holding out her hands across the gap between the tables to the wrists of Augustine and Christine.

"We thought with what went on that we should leave you guys to spend some time together," Augustine responded. It wasn't strictly true. Angelica hadn't invited them. She didn't know if she could. But that would have been Augustine's response if he was invited.

"Next time, maybe. But you are the detective, aren't you? We could probably do with you on this case. How long are you here for?" Andrea asked. Gerard had shifted closer to their edge of the table, gaining more interest in the conversation.

"We're here for a couple of weeks. I'm not a detective at the moment. I'm never a detective in Spain," Augustine replied awkwardly. His inner belief was that he was a detective every second of every day. But he had been told by Javi Jones he wasn't a detective here. He'd been warned by Christine to take it easy. And he was signed off from detective work back in the UK. This was probably as far away as Augustine had ever felt a detective since he'd been promoted to the rank.

"And do you do private work too?" Gerard asked, his Spanish accent making each word sound like it had been crafted to be as rounded as possible. Augustine smiled at the way he spoke. It reminded him of the tennis player Rafael Nadal, not that he could have said that in the town that produced a rival tennis player in David Ferrer.

"No. We're not allowed to carry out private investigation work alongside police work back home. It's against our principles," Augustine explained.

"But you're not in the UK."

"Rules still apply."

The conversation ebbed and flowed between the two tables. Sometimes they drifted back to their tables. Other times the chats went across the gap and included everyone. Angelica could sense a tension when Gerard and Andrea were talking alone. Her Spanish was good, getting better all the time, but it wasn't good enough to pick up on every word in a conversation. Andrea was born in the UK but had studied Spanish at school, college and then university. She was as fluent as Gerard who had lived here all his life. It wasn't the words that she sensed. It was the intonation. Spanish speakers had a certain pitch and cadence when they were speaking normally that sounded aggressive. But it wasn't. This was a notch above that normal pitch. Angelica could pick up on the difference. She wanted to know what it was but wasn't going to ask Andrea in front of Gerard.

The food finished, Augustine and Christine decided to take the kids for a walk along to one of the many playgrounds situated on the beach. He'd left plenty of cash for Angelica to settle the bill. She'd ushered them away, wondering if she could get the chance to find out what was happening between the couple on the table to her right. And she did get the chance. Around a minute after her table emptied, Gerard went to the bathroom. This was her chance.

"What's going on with you two?" she asked.

"Oh, something and nothing," Andrea replied.

"Well, forget about the nothing and tell me the something," Angelica went straight to the point. She'd had a couple of glasses of wine herself with the meal that evening. It had the same lip-loosening effect as it did on Carmen.

"He's trying to do something that I don't agree with."

"He's a man. Don't they always do that, Andrea?"

"This is bigger. You know he used to go out with Maria a few years back? Just before he met me?"

"Maria Valverde?"

"Yes, our Maria."

"I had no idea."

"Well, Angelica, he thinks that little Jose might be his child. The timelines are fuzzy. In the past he's asked her for a paternity test. She always refused. Now he's pressing for custody if Jose is his."

"Wow. I had no idea."

"It's been going on for longer than I care to remember."

"How do you feel about it?"

"I just wish they had sorted it out. It wasn't like Maria and Gerard was a secret. I've accepted it, why couldn't she?" Andrea asked.

"I always felt there was a little bit of tension between him and Maria. But I thought that was just Gerard's way."

"What was Gerard's way?" Gerard asked, getting back from the toilet without either of the women hearing him.

"Err, nothing," Angelica answered.

"I heard you talking. I asked you not to tell anyone," Gerard chastised Andrea.

"Sorry. Don't see what the big secret is. It's not like you're going to upset Maria now, is it?" Andrea asked. "If you're not the father then we can move on. If you are then we can move forward. But at the moment we're not moving anywhere at all."

"That's my business," Gerard replied with a look that confirmed the conversation was over.

16

The Boyles were sat on the balcony, the kids in bed in the room together just off where they sat. The night sky was a mix of clear and cloudy. Over the sea were the clouds, but they were high in the atmosphere and getting further away all the time. Across the land, particularly towards the Montgo mountain that dominated the landscape in and around Javea, you could see hundreds of stars. Living in Washington and seeing the night sky bleached by the constant yellow-orange glow from the Nissan factory, Augustine had partly forgotten what a sky full of stars looked like. He leant back in his chair and looked up as they spoke.

"Beautiful night," Christine said with a degree of impatience in her voice. She had tried many times that evening to steer the conversation away from the murder investigation. She had been unsuccessful every time.

"It sure is. I wish we could get nights like this in December back home," Augustine replied.

"I wish we could get nights like this at any time of the year," Christine rejoined, wondering if Angelica had grabbed hold of something too precious to let go of with moving to Spain.

"Lol," Angelica added.

"What's on tomorrow?" Christine asked, happy that they had put together a few sentences without referring back to Maria.

"Sunday is usually a quiet day in this part of the world.

How about a repeat of today but without the drama?" Angelica responded.

"Sounds good to me."

They fell silent. All they could hear was the snoring coming from the room. Tommy had a light snore, but it was persistent. Angelica wanted to get him checked out but had been persuaded by Andrea that it wasn't anything to worry about. Andrea had a calming effect on the way Angelica felt about bringing up Tommy.

"And if Javi gets in touch again, then we'll see if we can be any help," Angelica broke the silence. Christine's eyes rolled, missed by the other two who were giving each other knowing glances.

"How about…"

"Don't even bother, Gus," Christine interrupted.

"I'm thinking about how we can help without being involved. He wanted to know as much as possible about the people we first met on the cliff, you know, those who flagged us down in the car?"

"And didn't you give him what you knew?" Christine asked, topping up her wine glass before offering the bottle to the other two. Augustine nodded, Angelica too. Three freshly filled glasses under the stars. The night had a coldness that had suddenly arrived, apparently from nowhere. The women pulled their cardigans from the back of their chairs and slid their arms into them. Augustine would endure the change in temperature.

"Well, there's always more. I have some profiling sheets that I can access on the police website. Angelica, can you get your laptop?"

"Sure."

While Angelica was gone, Christine looked at Augustine. His demeanour was of a man who was determined to help. She could see that his main desire in life was to catch criminals. That's what floated his boat. This seemed like a good way to help without being drawn into danger. She would help them, hoping it got it out of their systems. She knew that there was every chance it wouldn't, but she was willing to give it a go.

Angelica returned with a laptop.

"Is it connected to a printer?" Augustine inquired.

"Yes. Wireless and all that. Bet you didn't know I'd arrived in this century, did you?" Angelica replied. Augustine ignored. He was busy clicking away at the laptop. He passed it over to Angelica. The printer needed a password to enable the document to come out. She obliged. There was no need to ask. She instinctively knew what was needed when he gave her back the laptop.

"Angelica, these are forms for police use only. I've saved it on your desktop. Can you please make sure you delete that for me? I mean permanently delete."

"Just a second."

Click, click, click.

"Done."

Angelica lied. She had no intention of deleting what might prove a useful tool in solving crimes. She had no idea when she might need this again. The excitement of the last few days had taken over. If it wasn't for the fact that the murder victim was a dear friend, she might have already been out there looking for a killer. If it wasn't for Tommy, she might have already applied to join the police.

"So, let's get our heads together and come up with all we remember about these people. Then I can take a photo of it and send it to Javi," Augustine explained.

"Best do that bit in the morning. It's almost midnight," Christine spoke.

"I have the feeling this man doesn't sleep much," Augustine responded. "But I will wait, just in case he isn't a robot."

The two women listened as Augustine explained how they brain-dumped all they knew about a suspect onto one of the forms he'd printed out. It was literally that – if you thought of something then you wrote it down. The more information on the page, the better. At some stage you would start interrogating the data to ensure you didn't have mixed information. For example, if you wrote, 'blue eyes.' At some stage, you didn't want to see, 'green eyes,' or 'brown eyes' elsewhere on the form. But initially it was just about putting down primary impressions on paper. The interrogation would start later.

"The most important thing is to write. Don't speak, don't look at what other people have written. I don't want anyone to be influenced by the thoughts of the other two of us. This is our own impressions, straight off the cuff. The idea behind it, is we know far more instinctively than we do when we engage our brain in deep thought about a subject. So, let's get some thoughts down on paper."

Ten minutes later, through a series of yawns, they had written between the three of them almost a full page of A4 paper on each of them – pretty good going for people they only saw for a few fleeting moments.

Angelica could see how this was a successful way of profiling people. She had written about their mannerisms, the way they made her feel and other details that weren't just about what they looked like. As a result, she had filled more than half the page herself.

Then they got to interrogating the data. Augustine read out each piece of information on the paper for them to listen to and decide if they agreed with it or not. The idea was they got the scrutiny of three minds without falling into groupthink by hearing what was said before they put their own ideas down on paper.

A further fifteen minutes, many more yawns and a couple of heated discussions later, they had a working document that they could send to Javi.

"I'm about done for the night," Augustine stated. Christine nodded, yawned and joined him on her feet.

"Night night you two," Angelica spoke, getting up and picking up the three wine glasses, all emptied of every last drop of their contents. "I'm shattered too. Time for bed."

All three pottered around, putting the last things in place before they went to bed. Augustine was cleaning his teeth, Christine tending to Nightingale, and Angelica washing the wine glasses.

They all retired to their rooms. But only two would sleep. One was far too excited for that.

17

Angelica covered the printer with a throw that she'd retrieved from the sofa. She wanted to print more profiling sheets. There was a burning desire for her to solve the murder of her friend Maria. And there was something else burning. It was a sense that the killer was in Andrea and Gerard's home the afternoon before. Something in her gut told her that she was in the company of a killer. At the time she'd ignored the feeling as it ticked away inside her. But the ticking had got louder and louder. She needed to get down on paper all she knew about the four women in her group of friends that was still alive, plus Gerard.

Wondering what someone else would write about her, Angelica started with a profiling sheet about herself. She picked up all the things she didn't like when she looked in the mirror. Angelica loved to anlayse the way she was viewed in the world. And it stood to reason that she would be a suspect just as much as they would. She knew for a fact that she hadn't committed the crime. But nobody outside her body would have the same knowledge. If she wasn't considered a suspect by Javi Jones then she would be surprised, even if she was some way down the list.

The notes on the page read, 'loner, doesn't have an alibi for most of the time on the days before Maria was killed, isn't a people person, doesn't have many friends in the community, has been close to violence through an ex, was close to the victim, has own car and access to the coast.'

Pretty damning if she was reading it from the outside. Now

for the rest of them.

Angelica wrote longer profiles for the others in the Girls On Tour group. She wrote down descriptions, feelings, what made them tick and details about encounters. Each sheet was filled front and back with details of her encounters with each of the people in the group, finishing with Gerard and Andrea, having got more information from them that evening.

Angelica tried to stay awake as long as she could. The words were flowing one second, she had stalled the very next. It was the tiredness kicking in. She fell asleep on the sofa with the sheets of paper all around her – on the floor, underneath her face, on the arm of the sofa and on the coffee table in front of it.

The room would still look like that when she awoke the next morning on the sofa.

18

Augustine stretched his arms as far as they could above his head. The headboard and wall stopped him getting a full stretch in that direction, so he angled his limbs upwards so he could get the full benefit of the stretch. The sunlight was tickling the edge of the curtains. They were blackout, but there was just the hint of brightness poking through at the sides.

He looked to his left and saw Christine on her back. He was reminded of a dream where he thought there was a train going past the window. Her snoring indicated what the source of that dream was. She snored only when she was on her back. Usually, he moved her. But he wasn't going to. Augustine had gone back to getting up early in the morning. Like his father and his aunt, Augustine was an early riser. It didn't bother him in the slightest. He'd met people who were upset to an extreme degree by the fact they arose early. But he just rolled with it. Wasn't much he could do but roll with it, in his mind.

Sliding out of bed carefully, as not to wake Christine, he managed to bang his foot on the wardrobe. He wanted to shout out in pain but that defeated the object of getting up quietly. He slid his feet along the floor, hoping that this would achieve the twin aims of making no noise and not banging his toes against any other furniture.

He was out of the room thirty seconds later and headed towards the living room. He'd eyed the sofa, the television and the throw the night before. His way of dealing with an early start was to sit in front of the television and vegetate for a while. It helped him get something in the way of rest without tossing and turning in bed, waking up the poor woman who was sound asleep next to him.

As Augustine entered the living room, he spied the throw on the shelving unit across from the sofa. Not where he expected it to be. As he got closer still, he could see that the sofa was occupied by his sister and many pieces of paper. He retrieved the throw, placing it down on his sister. She was still dressed from the night before, a nice light blue dress that she had worn to the pizzeria. It showed off her figure, revealing a thigh with the slit on the dress. Christine had commented on it. Angelica had smiled a smile that Augustine hadn't seen on his sister for a while, ever since she'd had to deal with Tommy's father.

Tucking the throw in, he spotted the profiling sheets scattered around Angelica.

'She's getting far too involved,' he thought to himself. 'I don't want to lead her down the same route I've travelled. It's ended up with me in hospital for months with some serious brain injuries, with my arm cut by a knife. I don't want that for my sister.'

As he stood over her, worrying about her infatuation with the murder investigation, the doorbell rang.

"Who is it?" he asked, not having the linguistic skills to ask in the local language.

"Suministro!" the reply came in a male voice. Augustine had no idea what they meant so opened the door. A man was stood there in a UPS uniform with a box in his hands. The box was around a foot square, with more parcel tape than Augustine had ever seen on one package in his life. If he'd been forced to guess, then he would say that this was the contents of two rolls of tape. By the way the UPS man was holding the box, it was heavier than it should have been for that size.

Augustine held out his hands. The man placed the box there and then clicked away at a handheld device that presumably needed his signature. It did. The UPS delivery man held it out to Augustine who squiggled something akin to his autograph. He found there was never enough room on these small devices to put his flamboyant signature.

"Nombre?" the man asked.

Still not knowing the language at all, Augustine thought back to the last time he received a delivery at home, in English. Now, what was it he did next?

His name! That was it. Augustine said, "Boyle."

The man seemed to recognize that and walked away tapping at the device.

As he turned around, Angelica was stood at his shoulder.

"Jeez. You gave me the fright of my life," he exclaimed, nearly dropping the box as he jumped out of his skin.

"Who is it?"

"Parcel for you," Augustine responded. They were the only two awake in the apartment. But Augustine knew Nightingale would soon follow them. This was his time alone with Angelica to ask questions about the case and her obsession with it. He wanted to help her lose that obsession and get back to her normal life – the one she called boring.

"Ange, what are you hoping to achieve with all of this," he asked, throwing his hand across the room to indicate the pieces of paper that still hadn't been tidied up.

Before she could answer, Augustine heard a retching noise coming from the other side of the room. He looked at Angelica, who had turned from her usual glowing self to someone who looked matt instead of gloss. She was going green. He ran across the room and got a glimpse of the inside of the parcel. Rotting meat was emanating a putrid smell up to his nostrils, about thirty seconds after his sister had got a whiff of the same thing.

He only saw it for a fleeting glimpse because she had bagged it with a carrier that was laid on the dining table. She flew out of the door and down towards the bins, which were situated on the street, opposite the apartment complex. The freshness of the morning was more than welcome. She needed some respite for her poor olfactory organs.

Two minutes later she was back in the apartment. Augustine had opened the windows and emptied two cans of air freshener, one from under the sink in the kitchen, the other from behind the lavatory in the downstairs WC. The manufactured smell wasn't pleasant but was far more preferable to the rotting meat that the parcel contained.

"Patty?" Augustine asked.

"I wish you'd stop calling him that," Angelica responded.

"Well?" he asked again.

"I can't think of anyone else."

19

The gang got out onto the street, ready for a day at the beach. The kids were particularly excited about this. Tommy had gone through the cupboards in the whole apartment looking for as many beach toys as he could find. The cupboards in the utility room were the most fruitful, yielding an extra three buckets for more sandcastle building and destroying.

Augustine had texted the images of the profiling sheets they put together on the people at the clifftop to Javi. He hoped it would help and that it would draw a line under things for a day at least.

He was wrong.

They hadn't travelled fifty yards when a car pulled up alongside them. Javi Jones held his head outside.

"Hola!" he smiled.

Angelica was the only one who had smiled back.

"How are we all today?" he asked. Christine kept walking with Nightingale in the pushchair with Tommy holding on to the handle. The siblings stopped to speak to him. They had told Christine about the package that had arrived earlier, but she hadn't experienced the unpleasantness of it. Neither had the kids.

"Not so good, Javi. While you're here, can we file a complaint?" Augustine asked. Angelica gave him a look that forced him to look away. She didn't want a fuss made of it.

"What is it about?" the Spanish detective asked.

"Angelica received a package in the post today. It wasn't very nice at all."

"What kind of package?" Javi enquired.

"It contained rotting meat. I was nearly sick with the smell," Augustine replied. Angelica was still giving the look, arms folded in a body language signal that told the pair of them she wasn't happy about the conversation.

"That's gross."

"Pretty disgusting."

"Where is it now?"

"In the bins over there," Augustine responded, nodding behind the car. Javi didn't turn around. He knew where the bins were.

"Do you think it could be related to what we've seen?" Angelica asked. Now that the cat was out of the bag, she might as well find out as much as she can.

"Wait there while I get my pad and pen," he said, leaning across the seat to the passenger side where the glove box contained his pen and pad. Augustine always said these were a detective's best friends.

"He said these aren't linked," Angelica whispered to Augustine. "What do you think?"

"He's probably correct. But I wouldn't rule it out," Augustine whispered back while Javi was shuffling around in his car, still looking for his items.

"Why?"

"Because we still have no idea what kind of sick mind we're dealing with."

20

After taking the scant details the siblings had regarding the UPS package, Javi revealed that he didn't just happen to be passing. He had visited there for a reason.

"I'd like to ask you a few questions about your relationship with Maria," he directed at Angelica.

"I've got a couple of minutes, nothing more," she replied, looking along the street to see Christine sitting on the edge of the marina with the kids. She had hold of Tommy around the waist, Nightingale was still in the pushchair. They were doubtless watching the small fish swimming in the clear water. It was one of Tommy's favourite activities. Angelica didn't walk this way if she was in a rush. She would never get to where she wanted in time because of Tommy's fascination with the fish.

Augustine stepped back to let the two of them speak. Then he had a question or two regarding the case himself. Maybe he would get answers. Maybe he wouldn't.

"How long have you known Maria?"

"A few years. Her son Jose and my son Tommy started playschool at the same time. She was already friends with the rest of the Girls On Tour group. Andrea welcomed me in, but Maria was probably the one who made me feel most accepted."

"And did you have any other relationship with her? Money? Investments? Clubs?"

"No, I only saw her with the other girls. We kind of move in the same circles because of the school and the fact that Javea's community isn't that large when you take away all the tourists and Madrileños."

"It can be quite a small place for such a large space, that's for sure. So, you wouldn't have seen her away from the rest of the group?"

"No."

"Never?"

"Never."

"And you aren't involved in any of her business interests?"

"I don't have the cash for that. You need to have deep pockets to be involved with Maria's businesses as far as I know."

"And what do you know?" Javi asked, becoming more intrigued in Angelica's knowledge of her friend. He knew they had an occasional drink as a group. He'd got that information from speaking to the rest of them. But he also got the impression that Angelica was an outsider, sticking to the side of the group rather than being an integral part of it. Now he was doubting that information.

"I know that if you have a business proposition in Javea, then Maria wanted to know about it. She had the time and patience to listen to every opportunity, no matter how big or small. Some people tried to take advantage of this but on the whole she was a smart cookie. You had to get up really early in the morning to get one over on Maria. But that doesn't mean she was immune to a scam. I'd heard in conversation a few times that she'd lost a chunk of cash on one deal or another. The perils of speculation, I guess. I wouldn't know about that. How about you Javi? Do *you* have the kind of cash for that?"

"No. But maybe you end up with money like that by taking a few risks here and there."

"Maybe."

"And can you think of anyone who might have a reason to kill Maria?"

The slayer question, Augustine thought. The one designed to extract the most from an interviewee. The question that put them on the spot. Augustine had asked this so many times that he had a good idea whether the person was wriggling on the spot, trying to point the finger elsewhere in an attempt to hide their guilt. Obviously, that wasn't the case with Angelica. She was no killer.

"Not at the moment. Augustine has sent you what we pulled together about the people who flagged us down and pointed out the body. But I don't think they were killers. They didn't have that feeling about them."

"You'll be surprised what a killer can actually look like or feel like. It isn't always what you expect. You say, 'not at the moment.' Might you have more for me later on? Over dinner perhaps?"

"No, I've got my family over. I couldn't possibly…" Angelica blushed, stuttered and stopped. She had nothing else to say on that matter.

Javi was blushing too. He wished he hadn't asked. The two of them stood there with bright red faces.

Augustine came to the rescue.

"Do you have the post-mortem yet?" he asked. Javi was more than grateful for the interruption.

"No. Still no coroner. We're a little closer to appointing one but these things take time in Spain."

"What do you have so far? How is the investigation going? Can I help?" Augustine didn't know how to frame the question, so he asked in three different ways. It didn't matter how he asked. Javi wasn't going to give anything away at that point in time.

"Nothing. There is nothing I'm willing to divulge at this point of the investigation. I still have a long way to go. I'm not at a stage where I can even speak to the press."

"The press?" Augustine asked.

"Yes. Over here we go to the local press for help pretty much as soon as we can in an investigation. There might be investigations where we can't do that, for strategic reasons. And there are some investigations where we have to leave out certain bits of information. But at the moment the press can't be of any help – not that they take that for an answer."

"If I can help then please drop me a line. It's far better than dropping by," Augustine responded with some irritation in his voice. He sensed that the man wanted a lot from them but wasn't giving anything in return.

As he walked off to join Christine and the kids, Augustine Boyle grew suspicious of Javi Jones. He certainly wasn't going to let his sister go out for dinner with the man just yet.

21

They were at the beach within fifteen minutes. It would have been ten if it wasn't for Tommy wanting to show his uncle Augustine the fish several times on the way. The day was cooler than the one before. Clouds added to the colder feel as the sun dropped behind them every now and again.

But for December it was still a good temperature for the seaside, an opinion confirmed by the number of people on the beach already. And it hadn't reached eleven in the morning.

"Great day for sandcastle building," Augustine said with a chortle. Tommy roared with laughter, Nightingale too.

The women set up the towels and blankets while Augustine took the kids down to the sea. It was cold, what Augustine's mother called 'fresh' in their youth. He was only ready for a couple of minutes of this freshness. But the kids were having far too much fun to be taken away from it by that point.

Tommy was jumping waves. As each one slid gently towards the sand, he leapt in the air, clearing the white foam at the crest of the wave before landing back on his feet the other side of the wave. Nightingale was motioning in the same way a yard or so behind, but her feet never left the ground. Augustine held her hands and gently lifted her over the waves. But after a few goes at this, she wanted the same freedom that her cousin was experiencing. She wriggled free and moved away from her father so he couldn't repeat the trick. Augustine sat on the edge of were the sea met the sand. He couldn't figure out if the tide was coming in or going out. The waves seemed to be equal one to the next.

The screams of delight from the two children under his watchful eye were repeated every fifteen yards or so along the beach from end to end. Kids were enjoying the relative warmth of the December sun, not perturbed by the intermittent cold brought about by the clouds.

After watching them from this distance for a good twenty minutes, he could feel the waves getting closer and closer to him. They started lapping around his ankles and then made their way up to the bottom of his shorts. He wasn't ready to get a wet backside, so got up, picked a child up under each arm and made his way back up the beach.

The kids didn't like this, wriggling to get free. But Augustine had a strong grip. There was no escape. He wanted to get back to the others, perhaps pick up a book and relax for an hour or two before lunch.

By the time they had got there, the other two had made scores of sandcastles. The wriggling stopped. The kid's attention had completely refocused from the sea to the sandcastles. Augustine could see the excitement glisten in their eyes as he put them down on the sand.

He sat down and reached for a book while a flurry of activity happened all around him. Christine filmed it on her phone, laughing all the way through the video. Angelica sat back and watched the waves hit the beach from a distance. She stared at nothing else for three minutes before scanning the beach from left to right. At the far left were the pleasure craft, heading out to the sea for fishing, diving or just meandering around. Then were the inflatable, pedaloes and the like, ready for hire even in December. Of course, there were far fewer options than in the middle of Summer. But the handful of choices were attracting some attention from the kids on the beach, pestering their parents to put their hands in their pockets.

Along from that, she saw families doing exactly what they were – setting up for a day at the beach. There was the odd dog on the beach. Strictly not allowed, but these dogs were the handbag variety, as Angelica called them. They sat in their owner's bag. The only issue with that as far as she could see was what happened when they needed the toilet. She didn't want to think about that eventuality.

As she moved her gaze across to her right, she could see the other mums from the Girls On Tour group, sitting together, chatting while the kids ran around in a game that was reminiscent of playing tag when she was a child but without the order. It seemed everyone was 'it' and everyone was also running away from 'it' at the same time. Confusing. The movement was mesmerising though, and Angelica watched them in wonder for a good few minutes. The flurry of activity was a nice contrast to the way her family were enjoying the beach. But she knew what she would rather be involved in. Peace and quiet all the way.

Angelica looked over at her brother and his partner. They were laid next to each other but somehow managed to use each other as a cushion. Christine was laid on his back, Augustine resting his head on her thigh. They were both deep in the book they had each brought to the beach. Augustine had a Kindle but didn't trust himself and his clumsy manner to not get it full of sand and rendering it unusable. The front cover looked dull and plain – the kind of book that Angelica overlooked. She definitely did judge a book by the cover.

She wanted a soulmate in the same way these two seemed to be for each other. All Angelica wanted when she was young was to be a mother. She had that. Tommy was all she had even dreamed of. But in her mind's eye, Angelica had always just assumed that there would be someone to share all of this with. And when Tommy's dad turned out to be someone she couldn't be around, she just went into survival mode. Coming out of that had been difficult, made even more difficult by the abusive messages. And now the parcel of rotting meat in the post. If she could trust someone again then Angelica felt she could get some of that back. And have a piece of what her brother was experiencing.

She imagined a man that looked like Jason Momoa from the *Aquaman* movies, but not quite that big. She didn't fancy ironing clothes that big and wondered what would happen to her flimsy-framed bed if a man of those proportions arrived on the scene. Her Jason would also be muscular, but not that much taller than she was. He would have an English accent, but maybe some of the darker Spanish looks. Dark hair, for sure.

Her daydream was broken by a scream. It sounded like it started with the voice of a child and continued with an older tone. She looked over in the direction of the noise and saw a flurry of activity with the Girls On Tour – this time far more frenzied. Augustine and Angelica jumped to their feet and ran over. As they got close, they were told to hold back.

"There's glass here somewhere. Please walk around the area, not through it," Gerard explained, his Spanish drawl pulling through in his rush to get the information out.

They walked around and found Briana making the same noise as before, over and over again. She held her son Marcus in her arms. He looked pale, like all the blood had been drawn from his face. And it might well have. Looking down his body, Angelica spotted the redness of blood, starting around his knee, all the way down to his foot, which was wrapped in a white towel, which was starting to spot with the deep red blood from underneath.

"What happened?" Angelica asked, trying to find out information but also distract Briana from her distress.

"It's Marcus. He's cut his foot," Andrea answered.

"Not you. Her…" Angelica replied, looking at Briana who was now starting to look as pale as her son. She wanted Briana to answer, to pull her out of her frenzy.

"Briana?" Angelica added, to ensure that there was no doubt who she wanted to speak to.

"He cut his foot. I saw glass sticking out of it. I… I don't know what to do."

Luckily, Delia knew exactly what to do and she had already run off to get her car. It was sticking its nose out at the end of the promenade, lights flashing.

Angelica helped Gerard wrestle Marcus from his mother

and then escort the pair of them to Delia's car. Angelica wasn't sure if Briana could have made the trip of only fifty yards for herself, let alone with her son in her arms. The shock had taken it out of her. Andrea volunteered to get in the car and keep an eye on the mother and child in the back while Delia drove them to the nearest health centre, a short drive away.

"I hope he's going to be OK," Augustine spoke.

"I hope they're both going to be OK," Angelica replied. "I've never seen her like that. We all care deeply for our kids. But Briana has struggled more than most with the protection element of motherhood. She's always trying to make money or save money. Not sure what she's up to now, but she did try to involve me in many of her schemes."

"And do you think money is a problem for her?" Augustine asked, the inner detective kicking in before he even had time to realise it.

"I believe so," Angelica responded.

"Maybe that's an angle we look from," he replied, watching his sister for a reaction. She didn't give one. Not one that he could read, at least.

22

"Oh, OK. I understand." Angelica was on the phone, back in the apartment later in the day. The fun of the beach didn't seem to hold quite as much joy after they had seen the injury to Marcus. They stayed for a little while longer, grabbed some lunch at one of the excellent cafes on the front and then walked back, taking in the many fish again for the sake of Tommy's excitement. The kids were under the watchful eye of the grownups and had to wear their sandals at all times.

"It's good that he's going to be OK. I did worry that with the number of veins and arteries in the foot, it might need emergency surgery. He's a very lucky boy that it's missed all of those vital bits and just gone through tissue," Angelica spoke down the phone. Walking around the apartment for the best signal. She had just changed mobile phone carrier and the signal wasn't quite what she'd expected. In certain parts of the apartment the signal was great. But in others it was patchy.

"I know. The doctor said it will be sore for some time. The stitches he's had in there will dissolve naturally. He did tell me how many stitches there were, but I didn't retain that information. When I heard the words that he's going to be fine, the rest just got lost in the emotion of it all," Briana explained at the other end of the line. Angelica could hear that the blood had returned to her body too. She sounded like the Briana she knew and loved.

"And did he say anything else?" Angelica asked. Something nagged away at the back of her brain, prompting her to ask the question.

"He did."

Angelica fist-pumped, celebrating that she had let her intuition run free and it had come up trumps. As far as she was concerned, it was another victory for the liberated Angelica returning to the surface.

But then silence.

"What?"

More silence.

"What did he say, Briana?"

"I don't know what to make of it. I can't really get my head around it."

"Well, tell me and we'll work it out together," Angelica reassured.

"He said that the glass had been deliberately sharpened. That it was meant to be a weapon, done on purpose rather than an accident. The piece of glass was like a dagger."

"You need to tell the police about this," Angelica explained.

"I'm not sure. I don't want to cause any trouble. Maybe the doctor was wrong. It could just as easily have been a mistake. Glass comes in all shapes and sizes, doesn't it?"

"And is a dagger one of those shapes and sizes?" Angelica asked, incredulously.

"It *could* be."

"And very likely isn't. What are you going to do?"

"I'll leave it for now and see what happens," Briana answered before hanging up the phone.

Angelica slammed her fist into the wall on the balcony, which was where she had ended up after chasing a signal throughout the call. The open air seemed to do the trick. She had managed to get a clear conversation. But she didn't believe the words she heard.

There had to be a reason Briana didn't want to take this any further.

23

Just as she hung up the call, her phone went again. Angelica pressed the green button to receive the call, believing it was Briana continuing the conversation. She'd had time to think. She'd come to her senses. She was ready to tell the police.

"Briana?"

"Angelica?"

"Yes, who's this?" she answered, realising it wasn't a female voice.

"Javi. Javi Jones. I have a few questions and need to meet you. Can you and Augustine come to the fish port now?"

"Get straight to the point, Javi, why don't you?" Angelica responded with a chuckle. She liked people who got straight to the point. She wanted more of it in her life.

"We'll be there in fifteen," she answered on behalf of her and her brother.

Christine didn't put up much of a fight. The kids were asleep, and she fancied a bit of the same herself. She curled up on the sofa. Augustine kissed her lightly on the forehead. Angelica swooned, wondering when her Jason Momoa lookalike would arrive in her life and gently peck her on the head.

They headed down the stairs and out of the apartment complex, hearing the faint splashes of water from the communal pool. The water there was probably as cold as that in the sea at the beach. And it was closing in on siesta time. The pool would be out of bounds within the next half an hour or so.

The roads were quiet. Angelica turned the car around and headed for the back road, away from the seafront. Although the journey along the front was infinitely more scenic, the road that ran parallel with it, about half a mile inland was much quicker. The dual carriageway allowed her to pass the other couple of cars they encountered along the road.

To their left were a series of unfinished apartment complexes – something to do with local planning laws, she had been told. If the building work started, then the planning permission endured. To their right were supermarkets galore. From the very Spanish sounding ones to the international ones and then the single English supermarket he recognised – *Iceland* to be precise. As they reached the end of the dual carriageway, the roundabout gave them a handful of options. One led back to the beach, one further inland and away from the peninsula Javea sat on, while the other took them to the port. This was where Javi Jones wanted to meet them.

"Steady on," Augustine commented as she took the roundabout in third gear, jamming her foot against the accelerator as they took the exit. The next roundabout was only fifty yards or so further on. They would be taking that one in third gear too.

Here, the shops turned from large supermarkets to small local affairs. The buildings all looked the same – yellow washed walls, terracotta tiled rooves and a large yellow-brown canopy. The only things that distinguished one from another were the signs above the doors and the goods on the inside.

They reached the busier part of the port a few seconds later. In the summer, these streets would be filled with hire cars from tourists who flock to Javea for the beautiful weather, amazing scenery, great places to eat and bouncing nightlife. It often took a few passes of every street to eventually find a single parking space. But in December there were plenty of choices. Angelica went along the streets and then turned left at the front, with the sea in sight, to head down to the fish port.

This is where the fishermen bring in their daily catch. Once nothing more than a fishing port, Javea had grown to be a major tourist attraction over the years. As more people visited for their holidays, a proportion of them wanted to stay. So, apartments went up, villas too. The population swelled so the fishing port became a quaint reminder of what was rather than being the whole place any longer. The fishermen landed what they could, according to EU rules and regulations, offering it for sale at the fish port. First dibs were reserved for the local restaurants. It was one of the reasons the food was so good – the fact that the seafood was swimming in the waters just off Javea on the morning before landing on your plate in the evening. And then, if there was anything left over, individuals could just rock up and buy what they wanted for homecooked meals.

Angelica parked the car up as near as she could. The fresh smell of sealife wafted through the air. A single man with a hose cleaned up the floor near to the fish port, keeping the place a pleasant experience for those who popped by to get their hands on something for their dinner.

Augustine jumped out of the car and looked around. Another part of Javea that he hadn't seen before; another new experience. He sniffed the air, and a smile ran across his face. He loved fresh seafood. Not as much as he loved pizza. But it wasn't far behind. The smell took him back to family holidays in Greece when they ate at seafood shacks on the beach. Something of that had stayed with him his whole life. He resolved to have seafood that night.

Angelica got out of the car with something else occupying her senses. Well, it was a lack of something that she was concentrating on. Javi Jones wasn't there. She followed her brother towards the fish port. But Augustine had stopped in his tracks, his head bowed.

"What's wrong with this picture?" he asked. She looked down at the same piece of ground as he was viewing. In one of the gaps between the large concrete slabs that made up the surface around the fish port was a piece of rope sticking out – the kind that you get on heavy duty fishing nets. He pulled. And pulled. The rope didn't give for the first few pulls and then came loose all at once. On the other end of the string was a key. He brushed off the soil that had surrounded the key. As he brushed, Augustine saw that there were markings on the key.

"What does it say?" Angelica asked, trying to get a view between her brother's hands. She felt like the kid sister again, trying to get a look at something her big brother was keeping from her.

"I can't see right now. Nothing that a bit of spit and polish won't reveal. Do you have a tissue?" he asked.

She dug in her handbag and came out with a small packet of tissues and an equally small packet of wet wipes.

"What mam goes out without these?" she replied with a smug look that she saved for occasions such as this.

"Thanks," he answered as he took a wet wipe from the pack in her left hand. He wiped away at the top end of the key, looking at the markings carefully as he did. He passed it over to Angelica who did the same with the other side of the key. They were working as a team. Their mother would be proud.

As the pair of them wiped away, taking it in turns to get the excessive dirt away from the key, a car roared its engine as it pulled along the road that connected the shops and restaurants to the car park and fish port.

The siblings looked up and saw Javi Jones. Augustine pocketed the key and brushed the dirt away with his shoe. Angelica looked at him and he put his finger to his lips. She turned around to the oncoming car and smiled.

24

Christine hadn't got very far into her siesta when the kids woke up. She could hear a constant din coming from the television downstairs. It sounded like police cars and a whole lot of action. She wanted to make sure Tommy hadn't pressed the button on the wrong channel and ended up watching something inappropriate. So, she got up. Nightingale had been bouncing up and down in the travel cot for some time by that point. It was rhythmical, which allowed Christine to blank it out while she was drifting in and out of sleep. But if she was getting up to see Tommy, she might as well get her daughter up and about too.

The television seemed to get louder as she descended the stairs. It wasn't the fact that she was getting closer. The remote had jammed between the cushions of the sofa, the 'volume up' button was depressed.

"Good job I got up when I did," Christine said to herself. With the noise in the room, nobody else would have heard it at any rate.

"Hi Tommy. How did your sleep go?" she asked. Tommy had his back to her, engrossed in building a tower with Lego bricks that would be pushed over as soon as Nightingale got near.

"I'm not Tommy! I'm a dinosaur!" he responded.

"Hi dinosaur. How did your sleep go?" she asked.

"ROAR!!!" he answered.

Christine looked out of the window laughing. The world looked like a great place to be. The blue sky was only broken by the odd cloud. The sun was beating down, the windows magnifying the intensity and making it feel like she was sat in a greenhouse.

It was time to get up and go out.

"Right kids, let's get ready."

"Ready?" Tommy asked.

"Yes, we're going for a walk. It's far too nice a day to be stuck inside," Christine stated. She bit her lip. She sounded more like her own mother every day. The things that parenthood did to you.

Ten minutes later they were outside. She had done the walk from the apartment to the beach a few times. She wanted to walk in a different direction. Nightingale was settled in the pushchair and Tommy was more than content to walk alongside. So, she just walked.

Whenever he recognised anything, Tommy gave her the lowdown from his perspective. They walked past the Mercadona supermarket and then onwards past parked cars and stacks of apartments. She had read before they left that Javea had an official population of around 33,000 – only around half of whom are Spanish. It reminded her of living in Durham, which she did for a short while as a child. That was around fifty percent student population. The streets swelled with people in term time and emptied when they all went home in the summer. Javea was the opposite. The place doubled in population size in the summer months – even though it felt like that extra number of people was way more than double the rest of the year.

She enjoyed the relative peace that the end of the siesta time brought. Families were stirring, shops were preparing to open again and even the birds in the trees seemed to have a relative calmness about them.

As they walked more, Christine spotted a pharmacy. Its flashing green light told her the time and the temperature. She slowed to look inside and see if it was any different to the ones back home – always good to have a handle on these places just in case she needed to visit one. Christine's mind was always working overtime with things like this. She didn't like the first time she had a new experience. It was all fraught with the unknown and potential upset. But once she'd done something once, she was totally at ease with it.

Tommy had wandered off to a playground right next to the pharmacy. He told his Auntie Christine that this was where he met Alfie for playdates. She was more than satisfied that the fence around the playground would keep him safely inside and she could see the only entry or exit from it. She intended for her and Nightingale to join him a few moments later.

As she got closer, the door to the pharmacy swung open violently and a woman barged out. A blonde woman with huge hair appeared. The pharmacist shouted out after her.

"Carmen…"

But there was no response. She obviously wanted to be out of there. Christine recognized the woman from somewhere but couldn't put her finger on it. She didn't retain information like this.

"Hi. Are you OK?" she asked as the woman walked with her head down, high heels clacking on the pavement as she marched away from the pharmacy. The man who had been shouting after her closed the door, looking both ways along the street.

Carmen ignored her. She didn't break her stride, didn't look up. Christine put herself and the pushchair directly in the way she was walking. The woman stopped.

"Are you OK?" Christine repeated. Neither woman recognized the other. They had only seen each other at a distance when Marcus cut his foot at the beach the day before.

Carmen grunted. "Suppose."

Christine waited. Carmen's head rose from gazing at the floor, and they made eye contact. Christine smiled. It wasn't reciprocated. But that was fine. They looked at each other for a few moments.

Carmen was stood much taller than Christine. The high heels were a large part of that. Christine was wearing her flat sandals. Perfect for a walk as far as she was concerned. Christine looked the woman up and down and spotted a huge bruise on her upper left arm. It was a handprint; she was sure of that. It looked painful.

"What happened to your arm?" she asked. The concern in her voice was obvious.

"Mind your own business," was the angry reply. And then the other woman walked off.

25

"Hola Javi. Lovely day," Angelica said as the Spanish detective got out of the car.

"Hola. Yes, lovely day," he replied looking up at the sky like it was the first time he'd noticed it that day.

"Why have you brought us here?" Augustine uttered, breaking the pleasantries and getting down to business.

"I have a theory. And this part of town is an integral part of it."

"Go ahead. Actually, first, tell me you've got a coroner on the case," Augustine prompted.

"No. Same old, same old. Budgets have got in the way. We're ready to appoint someone but we need clearance from the mayor. Nothing happens quickly in Spain, you'll find."

"So, I see. Tell me about your theory," Augustine responded.

"Tell *us* about your theory," Angelica added.

"Well, I have spoken to all of the friends of Maria Valverde. Present company included," he motioned towards Angelica with a nod and a smile. She could feel a warmth between the two of them. Augustine could feel it too. And while he didn't know enough about the detective, he wanted to pour cold water on it.

"Let's get down to business," Augustine steered the chat back to where it should be – on the business of catching a killer. He'd done this enough times to know every second counted, even if that wasn't the 'Spanish way.'

"Well, we have Andrea and Gerard. There is the small matter of the paternity claim here. I understand from the conversation I had with Andrea that this has been nagging away at Gerard for some time. Now Maria is 'out of the way,' he can pursue the claim without causing an issue between himself and Maria. That might be a motive to kill." Javi explained, looking around to ensure that the three of them were the only ones that could hear.

"Yes, it could. But he could have pursued a paternity claim when she was alive," Augustine spoke.

"And he didn't," Angelica added.

"Then there is Briana. She lost a stack of cash in a business deal with Maria Valverde," Javi said.

"Money is a big factor in many murders," Augustine added.

"But maybe not this one," Angelica countered. "Maria may have given Briana a bum steer with an investment, but she's savvy enough to know that you can lose everything on a speculative deal. I don't see her killing someone because she lost some cash. I don't think she's short of it."

"Agreed. Carmen and Maria don't have links that are particularly strong. I can't see a motive. There's no issue between the two women. Would that be fair to say?" Javi asked.

"As far as I'm aware," Angelica replied.

"And we have Delia. She was scammed, alongside Maria, a little while ago. Maria recommended a stock that was just starting to gain traction. Maria had heard about it from a friend of a friend. She recommended it; they both went heavy on it. There was no stock and all the cash disappeared overnight."

"Again, we're looking at the money angle. And I don't think that's the motive here," Angelica responded, assuming she knew her friends better than Javi did.

"I'm glad we're on the same page," Javi responded.

The siblings looked puzzled. They thought he'd brought them there to talk about a theory. And all he'd done was tell them that he didn't suspect the people closest to Maria Valverde. Before Augustine had the chance to bring this point up, Javi started talking again.

"There have been reports of people getting off these boats just before they reach the shore. Tourists told us about it in the summer. But there are hundreds of boats along this coast every day. We don't have enough people working for the police to sit and watch every boat coming in and out. And, of course, it's a place where the prying eyes of CCTV cannot reach. We believe that there is a people smuggling operation going on up and down this coast."

"This coast and every other one along the shore of the Med. If there's money then there's smugglers," Angelica added, remembering a documentary she'd watched a few weeks earlier. It told of the massive operation getting people from Africa and Asia across to Europe. The shores of the Mediterranean were the first part of the continent of Europe they set foot on.

"And this is where my theory rests," he said, waving his arm out over the sea in front of them. "We've been told of fixers in Europe who make all of this happen. They turn up here every now and again to check that their operation is still running as smoothly as it can. But they can work from anywhere on the planet. All they need is a phone and access to a Wi-Fi signal. We're talking a multimillion Euro operation run from a single telephone. It's the modern way."

"And what does this have to do with Maria?" Angelica asked, beating her brother to the punch by half a second.

"Listen, I don't have anyone else working with me. I don't have anyone to bounce ideas off. My colleagues are all sucked into the investigation of the bank robbery. Somehow a body in the sea doesn't interest any of them. I'm on my own. And that's why I called you here. I want to bounce this idea off you," Javi explained.

"Go ahead," Augustine answered as soon as Javi had stopped speaking. He wasn't going to let Angelica beat him this time.

"I think Maria Valverde was involved in the people smuggling operation here somehow. And those people you saw up on the cliff are part of it too. She is dead because she saw something or knew something she shouldn't have. How does that sound?" Javi asked.

"It sounds like you've had too much sangria," Angelica responded. She couldn't imagine her friend being involved in anything like this under any circumstances. But she also couldn't imagine her being found dead in the sea.

"Well, you agree with me that we don't have a solid enough motive for anyone close to her. The man who we believe is Jose's father is dead. She didn't have any enemies as far as we can tell. But there is unaccounted money in her financial affairs. More often than not that points to illegal activities. And when you deal with criminals, you can always end up bobbing up and down in the Mediterranean. Sorry to be so harsh," Javi added at the end as he saw how upset it was making Angelica.

"It's the first law of detecting a murder – we don't rule anything in or anything out. If we have to find the people smugglers to help, then we'll do that. So, we'll keep an open mind with the motive at the moment," Augustine said as he consoled Angelica. The death had just hit her hard.

"Well, I'm determined to prove that my friend isn't a people smuggler – even if that means I have to put another one of my friends in the frame."

26

"It's about time we changed these phones. I've been on the same SIM card for about a week now." His streamlined face pointed in her direction, looking for a response. He always wanted a response. His snake tattoo was in full view now he wore sandals.

She looked up at him from her seat. She had no idea why she'd chosen a lower seat than her companion. He was already a foot taller than her. The seat size made it look like they were father and daughter. He was a few years older than her but not old enough to make that a biological possibility.

"I'll get them when we go back to the room," she nodded in the direction of the hotel behind him. They were staying at the Hotel Parador, which had formerly been one of the chain of hotels owned by the Spanish state. But it had nothing that indicated a state-run enterprise. It was plush, uber comfortable and at the more expensive end of the budget for hotels in the area. She picked a small stone from her sandals and threw it in the direction of the bushes, which were being watered by an automatic sprinkler. A small bird scooped down to check it out, mistaking the movement for an insect. It flew off after discovering it was only a stone.

"And we need to make some money today. How about making a few calls later this afternoon? Just because these people have a siesta, doesn't mean it's a siesta everywhere in the world," he added, again needing a response.

"I think there's a more pressing matter today," she challenged. He knew it as well. But he'd been trying to avoid it.

"The woman?" he asked.

"You know fine well the woman," she answered with an impatience. He was still trying to avoid the conversation. She flashed her blue eyes at him. It was time for him to explain.

"Which woman?" he asked, prolonging the agony.

"She was around five foot eight, light brown hair, although I can't tell you if that is natural or out of a bottle. She confronted you in the street about a deal that had gone wrong. I told you a million times that we don't get involved with members of the ordinary public. They don't have the same appetite for loss as we do. If they lose a Euro, they go mad. Where the people we usually deal with only get angry when they lose it all."

"Oh, that woman. She had to be dealt with."

"So?"

"So, I dealt with her."

"Do I need to know the details?" she asked, the wind picking up and blowing her blonde hair over her eyes. She missed the look he gave her. It was supposed to transfer the message that he was in charge. But even if she did see the look, it wouldn't have changed anything.

"I'm going to get the SIM cards now. We were really close - too close for comfort up there on that cliff. The police must have arrived only minutes after we left. I can't be that close to losing all of this again."

She returned five minutes later with the SIM cards for their burner phones. Then they proceeded to make telephone calls, pushing deals and making their money. The sun shone hard on them, his face turning redder by the second. But he didn't care. This was the life – making money off the back of other people. Every now and again someone had to get hurt. Just as long as his pain wasn't much more than a bit of sunburn every now and again. He could handle that.

27

The food was laid out in front of them. Even though Augustine had fancied going to a restaurant for seafood, the homecooked platter was even better – mainly because it had been cooked with love by his sister.

"Thank you, Angelica," Augustine and Christine chimed in unison.

He looked across at the table. There were fresh langoustines, blushing a deep pink and ready to be torn apart, smothered in melted butter. The spaghetti vongole was one of her specialities. She'd never made it until she arrived in Spain and got inspired by the fresh clams on offer. The local Italian restaurants always cooked it with linguine, but she found spaghetti was more readily available, even though Javea had more supermarkets and food shops than she'd bothered to count. The bread was fresh and warm, the steam escaping when he tore the loaf apart. This with aioli would constitute a large proportion of his meal. He loved the garlic mayonnaise, consuming tub after tub of the stuff whenever he was near it. And to top it all off, there were fresh turbot, bought from the fish market while they were there. He was in seafood lover's heaven.

The food was consumed at a rate of knots. The kids were plated up first, making sure that there were no bones in the fish. Nightingale had developed her father's taste for aioli and spooned it into her mouth rather than dipping her food in it. Then the adults tucked in, putting huge spoonsful of each food on their oversized plates and eating heartily.

"Amazing food Ange. I guess you've learned to cook like a local," Augustine joked. Her cooking had been the butt of many jokes when they all lived in the North East of England. She could get by, but there was no skill or finesse involved. But now she was cooking amazing meals like this with ease. She didn't dare tell him that a cookery class was the reason behind it.

"I always had it in me. Just needed the sunshine and the right ingredients for it to come out," she replied with a knowing smile.

"Well, I'm glad it has," Christine added, wiping away the food from Nightingale's chin before looking at Tommy's face to see if it needed the same attention.

"And it seems the inner detective has come out too, Ange," Augustine spoke.

"I'm glad you noticed," she responded.

"Well, I've been meaning to speak to you about it. Why the fascination with the case?"

"Well, it's my friend. She deserves justice," Angelica replied.

"Every victim of crime deserves justice," Augustine added, he knew that far too well. The people who he couldn't deliver justice for still haunted him in his dreams. He was still driven by the twin aims of removing them from his dreams and making the world a better place for Nightingale to grow up in.

"And who better to look into it than someone who knows

her well?" Angelica enquired.

"Well, we have rules relating to this back at home. We can't investigate crimes that we're linked to. I couldn't investigate the death of a family member or friend. Not officially at any rate."

"Well, it's a good thing we're not back at home. And I'm not investigating officially. That's down to Javi. And it looks like he trusts me with the information he has. So, I'd say that makes it fine," Angelica responded, folding her arms at the end of the sentence. It was a trick she'd learned from their mother. It indicated, 'conversation over.' Augustine was willing to let it slide but vowed to himself that he would do anything and everything to protect his sister from harm.

"Anyway, I've put so much work into this," Angelica added, reaching to the desk behind her, grabbing a file and slamming it down on the table.

Augustine shuffled his chair up next to her and opened the file. It was the profiling sheets of the people involved in the investigation. Angelica had been adding information to the pages she had written out a few nights before. She had even got photos printed of the people on her camera roll, stapling them to the front of the first page at the top right. Augustine had seen sheets like these before. He compiled them in exactly the same way.

Christine got the kids down and started clearing the table. She could see the same dogged determination in Angelica that frustrated her with Augustine at times. She was going to let them get it out of their system. Christine was resigned to the fact that a large chunk of her holiday would be punctuated with the investigation. She could feel for Angelica. She had been through the same emotions when her friend Betty had died. It was the first time she had met Augustine, their very first date. And by the end of it, Betty was dead. She wanted to investigate, to catch the sick person who had killed her dear friend. But she left it to the professionals.

Walking backwards and forwards with plates of food, letting the discarded langoustine shells drop into the silver pedal bin in the otherwise all-white kitchen, she made a pile of plates by the side of the sink. The hot tap was running, slowly filling the sink with water, bubbling up as it hit the washing up liquid in the bottom of the basin.

She leaned over in between Augustine and Angelica to gather the last of the plates and looked down at the piece of paper they were deliberating over. When she looked at the images, she recognised the woman as the one running out of the pharmacy.

"I saw her today," Christine uttered.

"Saw Carmen?" Angelica asked.

"Yes, that's her name. She was running out of the pharmacy. The pharmacist was shouting after her, but she wasn't happy. She walked away, not even looking back," Christine explained.

"That's our Carmen. She does that a lot," Angelica said.

"I know. She did it to me a few seconds later. Seems like she's pretty preoccupied at the moment."

"So, what did you do to incur the wrath of Carmen?" Angelica asked in a joking manner.

"All I did was ask if she was OK."

"Was that it? She usually takes a bit more provoking than that, even on a bad day," Angelica asked.

"I did ask about the bruise on her arm. She had a massive bruise in the shape of a hand on her upper arm. It looked like it was quite painful. I did wonder if that was what she was in the pharmacy for. But she should know there isn't a great deal you can do for a bruise," Christine responded.

"She's never had bruises before. Not that I've ever seen. She gave no clue about why she might have it?"

"Nothing. She clearly didn't want to talk about it. How are things at home?"

"That's just the thing. I don't know. But I do know she wasn't totally happy with Alberto. He loves her but wants far too much control for my liking. Carmen isn't the beauty queen he married. And she can be liable to fly off the handle from time to time. I don't know whether he walks away from that or responds in kind."

They all looked at each other.

"Are you sure this is the woman you saw?" Angelica asked.

"One hundred percent."

28

Alberto walked out of the en-suite bathroom in the mansion he and Carmen shared. She was filing her nails. He made his money from selling Spanish porcelain to the rest of the world in the days before the internet. Nowadays, it was easy to click a few buttons and find pretty much anything you wanted from any corner of the globe. But go back twenty years and this wasn't the case. Alberto believed in the quality of Spanish porcelain for tiles and bathroom furniture. He used this passion to jump on a plane and speak to as many people as possible about the product. At first, he was a middleman, selling the wares of the factories in and around the town of Javea where he was born and grew up. But after a while, he invested in factories, eventually taking ten of them over as the sole owner. Needless to say, the floor in the mansion was decked in tiles made in one of his factories.

"Whoa! What's that on your arm?" he asked as he saw Carmen on the bed, alternating between touching her bruise tentatively with one arm while filing her nails on that hand with the other. The blade of the nail file glistened in the spotlights recessed in the ceiling. It made the whole room shine. But the nail file was the one thing that shone out about all others. She hadn't noticed he was there until he spoke.

"What the hell, Alberto?" she screamed.

He knew this mood. It started with the shouting and then went into the self-pity. He really wasn't in the mood for it.

"I was just asking," he replied with his hands outstretched to indicate he meant nothing by it. He was just concerned about the love of his life.

"Well don't ask. If I want to tell you then I will. But right now, I can do without your moralising. Can you give me a few moments peace at least once a day?" she shouted at the top of her lungs. The wine she'd drunk to numb the pain from her arm was well into her system. A bottle and a half of some Spanish red wine she'd been persuaded to buy at the bodega. She tried to get to her feet and wobbled a little. Alberto held out his hand to steady her.

"Don't you dare touch me!" she shouted. It was as much as he could take. She was up on her feet, throwing shoes at him when he left the bedroom.

He also left the home.

Alberto worried as he walked into the street, leaving Carmen behind, about their future. She wasn't the person he fell in love with when they first met. It wasn't the way she looked. He didn't care about that. It was the way she acted.

Alberto called a solicitor friend, an expert in Spanish divorce law. He wanted to know where he stood.

29

Christine put the kids to bed after tidying up the dinner table. Her and Augustine would do the washing up later. Christine felt a pique of excitement that she'd contributed to their unofficial investigation. She'd got a bit of the bug that had consumed Angelica over the past few days.

As soon as the kids were in their beds, she poured herself a glass of Rioja and joined the other two at the table. She leafed through the profiling sheets Angelica had put together, marveling at the detail she'd managed to come up with even though she was untrained.

Christine longed to get back to work. She loved being a mother and spending just about all her waking hours with Nightingale. Their daughter was a delight to be around, almost always happy and inquisitive beyond belief. But Christine wanted to be part of something in a work sense. She wanted the bug that Angelica had found. She just didn't want to spend her whole time investigating the deaths of other people. There was already one person with that role in the home. One was enough.

"There's so much work in this, Angelica" Christine said, still flicking through the notes. Her organised brain wanted to highlight in different colours so she could reference the information quickly. But it wasn't her work to mark up.

"Thank you. I thought the best way to get all of this out was to write and write until there was nothing left to write. I think it's easier to take away than it is to keep adding," Angelica replied, sipping her own glass of Rioja. Between the three of them, they were already halfway down the second bottle. A third would soon follow.

"Well, I can see how this would get you going. I really like the structure behind it. I think that it's a good thing you two are working together on this. It doesn't look like Javi Jones is getting much help from the station," Christine spoke.

"I thought you were dead against us looking into this?" Augustine responded. He was a little tipsy, being responsible for most of the red wine that had been drunk at the table.

"I know, but I'm starting to have second thoughts. You guys are good at this, I can see that. And, as I said, Javi needs some help or the killer will get away with this," Christine explained.

"OK. But Ange, I need you to be safe here. No murder investigation is without its dangers. Remember what happened to me a few years ago. Brain injuries are no fun at all," he explained.

Angelica nodded.

"And, as for me, I can't get too involved. I'm supposed to be here resting. We'll help Javi but stay in the background."

"That's not like you, Gus," Christine responded.

"I know. But I dread to think what Marie would say if she found out about this."

30

Early the next morning, Joy Fredriksson was walking her dog, a young Labrador that seemed to never want to grow up. The energy levels hadn't waned as the dog got older. She guessed that he was in its late teens, early twenties or even older than that in dog years. She'd anticipated that it would have settled by now. But there was no sign that Fluffy the Labrador would ever calm down into an adult dog.

Fluffy ran amok when she was in the quiet side streets, sniffing around bins and generally chasing anything that moved – whether it was alive or blown around by the wind. As a result, Joy stayed away from the main roads. The dog wasn't streetwise at all. She feared that it would end up under the wheels of a car if she let it loose near any amount of traffic.

She walked up near the mansions on the hills of Javea because each mansion was pretty much the only things at the end of its particular street. That meant only one household of cars to go in and out of there. It meant Fluffy would be safe.

The dog was mounting a dumpster like it could get the thing pregnant. Fluffy hadn't been neutered. She didn't believe in altering the true nature of an animal to suit her human needs. But at times like this, Joy wished that she'd put him through the procedure. It would save an awful lot of embarrassment.

Joy's usual tactic was to let him go about his business for a minute or so before grabbing him by the collar and taking him back to the street for a walk. Otherwise, she would spend her whole walk in a single standing position and Fluffy would come back home with as much energy as he left. And the point of the walk was to burn off as much of that as possible.

A minute or so into Fluffy's dumpster humping she decided that enough was enough. She heard someone else over the brow of the hill and the last thing she wanted was the embarrassment of her dog mounting an inanimate object.

Joy skipped over to the bin. She loved to skip. That was another reason she walked in the more secluded areas of Javea. Nobody understood why a fifty-three-year-old woman was skipping. She just enjoyed it. Her whole demeanour was that of someone much younger than the number of candles she blew out on her birthday cake. She wore as close as she could afford to the latest fashion, bought from the Zara store in the nearby Ondara shopping centre. She wore her hair in pigtails, just like she did at school.

"Fluffy, come here," Joy demanded, knowing that he paid no attention to her whatsoever. She knew that she'd have to get up close and personal with someone else's trash to drag the dog away.

As Joy got closer to the bin, the smell was different to what she normally experienced when dragging Fluffy away from rubbish dumpsters. It was a human smell rather than a bin smell. Strange.

The first thing Joy noticed was the handle of a nail file sticking out of the bin. She screamed when she realised that the nail file was sticking out of the ear of a man. Within seconds, the other person who she'd heard over the brow of the hill was stood beside her.

He put his hand in his pocket and it came back out with a phone.

"Police. My neighbour is dead. His name? Alberto Sintesa."

31

Angelica sat in shock at her home. She'd received a call from the neighbour, a man she'd met a few times called Pedro, who said that Alberto had been found dead and Carmen was being taken away by the police. He'd asked Angelica if she could come over and look after their daughter Tiana. Augustine, Christine and Nightingale had gone out for the day, leaving early to see the sights of Guadalest. The beauty of the mountain town is one thing. The surrounding scenery is something else altogether. The turquoise lakes that can be seen from the summit of the town were enchanting.

Tommy and Tiana were playing. She had taken the lead, dressing up her Barbie doll in clothes that weren't too dissimilar to the ones her mother usually wore. The Barbie had huge hair. It looked like it had been backcombed. Tommy had an Action Man doll, dressed up in a tuxedo. It was a gift from one of Angelica's great aunts who didn't know about her desire to give him non gender specific toys. But she guessed it would do no harm. The first time she saw Tommy pick up some Lego and fashion it into a gun, she wondered whether she was fighting a losing battle with it all.

She listened halfheartedly to the kids playing. Tiana had named her doll Carmen, which made Angelica prick her ears up.

"Why can't you be like all the other daddies?" she asked.

"I want to be who I am. Not who they are," Tommy replied via his Action Man, who he'd named Superbullet – not really in keeping with either Tiana's game or his mother's ideals.

They played again for a while. Angelica tuned in and out of what the kids were doing. Her thoughts were torn between making sure they were safe and what had happened to Alberto. If it actually was Carmen that killed him then might it also have been Carmen who killed Maria?

"I'll get you kids a drink," Angelica said as she got to her feet and walked to the kitchen. She grabbed the fresh orange juice from the fridge (what else would you drink when you're so near to Valencia?) and poured two beakers.

As she walked back into the room, she heard Tiana say, "My name is Carmen and I like to hurt people. Who will I hurt next?"

Angelica returned to her deep thoughts. Surely it couldn't be that one of her friends had killed another.

32

On his return from Guadalest, Augustine received a call from Javi Jones. He told Augustine that Carmen had been arrested. He'd asked if Augustine could be a 'consultant' on the case. Augustine immediately knew what that meant. It meant that Javi Jones wanted to get on and interview Carmen but didn't have anyone else to sit in with him for the interview. It wasn't a tactic that Augustine would use himself, but he was aware that it was something available to him if needed. He guessed that Spanish policing procedures allowed the same kind of backup. It meant that the ticking clock you had to interview a suspect didn't tick out while you waited for someone to sit in with you. Interviewing one to one was forbidden. It was no more than one word against another, even with voice recordings or video recordings. And it opened up the police officer to accusations of harassment. The last thing they needed.

Augustine assented to the request and returned to the police station in the port area of Javea once he'd dropped Christine and Nightingale off at the apartment. He was met outside the police station by Javi Jones, who went through what they had and what they would do from there.

Augustine was there, as more of a witness to the discussion than anything else. He would be introduced at the start of the conversation but was expected not to say anything at all throughout. If he had something to add, then he was to make a note and speak to Javi in the recess. A recess was always structured into interviews like these to give the interviewee time to clear their head and the interviewer the opportunity to sound out their line of questioning. Better to double check and ask the right questions than let the suspect walk away with outstanding issues to resolve.

They entered the police station, a dark affair that was probably welcome in the heat of the summer sun. But as it was winter, the corridors just felt intimidating rather than secluded. Augustine wondered if there was an element of intimidation built into the design. After all, it was built during the Spanish Civil war, when interrogation and suspicion were rife. It would be much easier to scare someone into a confession if they were already scared by the building itself.

The first room on the right was where Carmen sat. The two men joined her. In Spain, the interviews would always be transcribed in Castilian. But they would be conducted in the language of the accused. The detectives spoke a variety of languages, which made it easier for them to change language to suit rather than wait for a translator. Carmen had waived the right for legal representation. She looked like she was nursing a hangover. Augustine hoped that this hangover wasn't part of the decision-making process in turning down a lawyer. She might need one. Her husband was dead, and she was the prime suspect at that point in time. And it would be easy for the detective to link this death to the one of Maria Valverde. Both known to Carmen. That was a big start in any murder case. It was still the fact that most murders were committed by someone the victim knew well.

"Carmen, this is Augustine. He is a consultant to the

Spanish police and will be sitting in with me. Let me check again that you don't want a lawyer?" Javi asked. His voice was less singsong, more procedural than usual. The Welshness had disappeared for the time being.

She nodded her head, not looking up from the ground. The roots of her hair were showing a darker brown than the blonde on top. Her makeup was streaked down her face. She had obviously been crying. Augustine wondered if the guilty cried.

"For the record, please note that the suspect declined the offer of legal representation," Javi spoke into the microphone. It was the first time Augustine had noticed it. The mic stuck out from the wall. He assumed that the recording equipment was somewhere on the other side of that wall. If it was him conducting the interview, he'd much rather have seen the device, pressed the buttons himself, seen the red light on that indicated everything was being documented.

"Carmen, can you tell us how Alberto ended up in the rubbish bin outside your home with a nail file through his ear into his brain?"

She looked up, like she was confused with the words coming out of his mouth. He repeated the self-same words. She watched his lips intently, like it would help her to understand. Then she shrugged.

"For the record, the suspect has indicated that she doesn't know," Javi explained to the mic.

"Where were you last night?" he asked, tapping the desk that sat between them. Augustine looked at the desk and wondered how many interviews had happened there. He wondered how many guilty people had got away with it – and how many innocent people had been framed for a crime they didn't commit.

"I went to bed. I didn't feel myself over the last few days, since Maria died. I've drunk too much every day since. So, I've been falling in and out of sleep all day long and all night long. It's all a bit of a blur," she responded, slurring her words like she was still drunk. But she wasn't. Augustine recognised the reactions. It was grief mixed with confusion. It made the brain fuzzy.

"When did you last see Alberto?" Javi asked, leaning in. It was a tactic to make it feel like it was just the two of them talking, that the microphone was an ornament rather than a tool of the police.

"We had a row last night."

"What did you argue about?" he asked.

"I can't remember. I think he was being loving and caring but I really wasn't in the mood for it. I shouted at him, and he walked out."

"Was there any more than this? Just a shout? Did either of you raise your hands to the other?" Javi asked, keeping up the flow of the conversation so it seemed a natural chat rather than a police interview. Augustine liked his style – even more impressive as it wasn't his native tongue.

"I threw some things at him. I don't think any of them actually hit the target," she replied nervously.

"And what did you throw? Was it a nail file?" Javi enquired, pressing the buttons, ramping up the pressure.

"I was filing my nails when we started. How did you know?" she replied with a question.

"Just a hunch," Javi responded. "Shall we leave it there for a while?"

Javi and Augustine got up and walked to the door. Augustine knew this tactic. It was to get to a pressure point and then let her sweat. While they were out of the room, she was supposed to start digging a hole that she couldn't get out of. But something didn't feel right. That tactic only worked if the person was guilty. This wasn't clear with Carmen. Augustine had a few questions for Javi when they were on their own. But he had one for her first.

"Do you want a cuppa?" he asked over his shoulder.

"No, I'm alright," she responded, deep in thought. Maybe Javi was right. Maybe she was digging her own hole.

"What do you think?" Javi asked as soon as the door was closed behind them. Augustine was sure that she could still hear, so he motioned along the corridor for somewhere more private. Javi led him outside and sparked up a cigarette.

"I'm not sure," Augustine said, starting the conversation again.

"Not sure about what?" Javi asked between puffs.

"I'm not sure if she killed her husband."

"Well, he didn't travel far. He was found in the dumpster right outside their apartment. Whoever killed him, we have Carmen at the moment as the last person who saw him alive. And I'm sure in the UK it is the same as here – that often points to the killer."

"Often, but not always, Javi. What else do we have? What are you going to ask her next?"

"I'm going to ask *her* to talk. The way I usually go about this is a load of quick questions, where quick answers are necessary. Then I ask them to give me the full account of the time in question. This is where I can pick holes in their timeline, exposing their lies."

"And what if she doesn't lie?" Augustine asked.

"We'll cross that bridge when we come to it. Is that the right expression?"

"Yes, Javi. That's the one."

Javi threw the last third of his cigarette on the floor and stamped on the embers. He looked up at the sky as if divine intervention might be needed and then walked back into the station. Augustine did the same – looked up at the sky and followed. But he was looking for an escape. Not for him, but for Carmen. Something inside told him that she wasn't their killer. Maybe the next few minutes would persuade him otherwise.

"Carmen, please tell me everything that happened last night." Javi asked.

"Starting when?" she asked, wondering when 'last night' started and ended.

"Well, it was a normal evening. We had dinner together, the three of us. Our happy little family. It started with some bread and aioli then chicken, salad, and boiled potatoes. It's our go-to meal when we're busy. And we're busy people. After dinner, I watched some television with Tiana. She's into *Power Rangers* at the moment for some reason, so I sit with her for one episode. It's about all I can handle. If she wants to watch more then I let her do that on her own. While we watched this, Alberto was tidying up. He gets good time with Tiana in the morning and at the weekend, so he does the chores while I get some quality time with our girl in the evening. He's good like that. So, we watched, and she was yawning throughout. Tiana isn't like other kids. When she's tired, she wants to go to bed. She doesn't hanker to stay up late or anything like that. She just says, 'goodnight,' and goes to bed. I got downstairs just as Alberto was finishing up. He was distracted – he gets like that sometimes. So, I went upstairs, had a shower and decided I would pamper myself. I took ages on my hair, filed my nails, that kind of thing. Anyway, I was in my own world, doing my own thing. Alberto came out of the shower and started questioning me," Carmen explained, all without drawing breath.

"Questioning you about what?" Javi asked.

"This," Carmen said, taking her jumper off and exposing the bikini top underneath. She also exposed the massive bruise on her arm which was now mature enough to be showing yellowness around the edge as well as an array of greens, blues, browns and purples across the middle.

"For the record, the suspect has shown us a bruise in the shape of a hand mark, approximately two to seven days old," Javi said to the microphone, reminding Augustine it was present again. Even though he conducted these interviews all the time at home and was always aware there that he was being recorded, something about being abroad in an unfamiliar room had wiped the normality from the situation. He was a tourist in so many ways.

"And how did you get this bruise?" Javi asked, wanting to prod it with his finger but resisting the urge.

"I don't remember," was the curt reply from Carmen. Not exactly shining a light of innocence on her but stopping the light of guilt from shining too.

"Surely you remember a bruise of that size appearing on your arm. It must have hurt at the time it happened, no?" Javi enquired.

"No idea. I've drunk a lot lately, especially since Maria was killed, I don't recollect it happening. Anyway, I was filing my nails with one hand, touching the bruise with the other. Alberto came out and started asking questions about it – the same as you are now. I lost it. I don't know and I can't remember. I don't want to be grilled about it. I shouted at him, told him to get out and started throwing things at him. He left the room and I think he left the house."

"Where did he go?"

"I have no idea. He does that sometimes. He goes out and doesn't come back – sometimes for hours. Just answer me one question. How come you knew I was filing my nails?"

Javi shoved an image across the desk. The tears flowed down Carmen's cheeks and onto the image. The paper started to blister where the wetness of her tears puddled. Augustine leaned over and saw an image of Alberto with a nail file sticking out of his ear.

"Did you do this?" Javi asked.

"No," Carmen answered through sobs of tears.

"What else happened that night? After he left the room?"

"Nothing. I got on with my pampering, he left. I haven't seen him since. I'll never see him again."

"Do you have anything else to add?" Javi asked. There were no gaps in her story. He was beginning to have the same doubts as Augustine. Whether he had doubts or not, he didn't have enough to charge her with. The only alternative was to let her go. But he'd keep an eye on her. She was told to go nowhere. They were always told that.

33

Augustine and Javi sat in the interview room after Carmen had been released. He wanted to go back home to his family, but Augustine needed a few moments to unwind. He's always been like this. The commute home from work was his chance to wipe away the thoughts and memories of a hard day chasing murder suspects, storing the information away to be retrieved on his next commute into work again. He knew from experience that it took anywhere between quarter of an hour and half an hour for this process to happen. And the drive back to Angelica's apartment was five minutes max. So, he wanted to just sit there and do nothing for ten minutes at least. Javi was more than happy to sit in silence with him.

They had been there a few minutes when a head appeared around the door.

"Boss, we have the post-mortem from the woman found in the sea," the head uttered in a broken English accent that suggested neither English nor Castilian was her first language.

Javi nodded at her and then nodded at Augustine. He smiled, indicating that he had the few minutes needed to go through the report, or at least listen to Javi go through it as it would inevitably be in the native language.

Javi read aloud, "The deceased was found to have suffered from hypernatremia."

"Which is?" Augustine asked. This was a new one on him. He'd heard of victims dying from stab wounds, blows to the head, drowning and many others. But he didn't even know what that word meant.

"Salt poisoning. It isn't unusual here, because we're surrounded by salt water and people spend their whole life in and on the sea. It's not common – but it's not like it has never happened before," Javi explained, rounding his vowels like a Spaniard again.

"Interesting. So, is that what killed her?" Augustine asked.

"The report says that it is very likely she was alive when she was thrown into the sea. The extensive bruising on her left side indicate that she was thrown from some height, maybe the cliffs."

"So, what killed her? The salt? The drop? The bruising?" Augustine asked like an impatient child wanting to know the answers. Javi scanned to the bottom of the report, looking for the final word that would give the answers and shut the man up.

"Give me a second… Here it is… There was a struggle, the person who threw her in the sea may have marks on their body from the struggle. Maria Valverde was found with a punctured eardrum, probably from an implement with a relatively large blade such as a small kitchen knife or nail file."

The pair of them jumped from their seats and ran towards the door and looked for the woman they had finished interviewing minutes earlier. Carmen was long gone.

34

Angelica looked at her phone. She had a feeling it wouldn't be a nice message. And when she looked, the feeling she had was spot on. She read it across a few views. She was sitting in the front room with Christine and the kids and didn't want to alert anyone else to the fact she was being sent the most menacing message yet. Reading only a few words and then taking a break from the text for a minute allowed her to keep her calm on the outside, even though on the inside she was reaching boiling point.

Augustine was still out. And Angelica felt like he was the only person she could confide in with these messages. He had told Javi Jones, but that was different. That was in an official sense. But in terms of having someone to talk it over with, her brother was the one and only.

She had lost a great deal of faith in humanity as she suffered abuse at the hands of Tommy's father, Patty. The man was clever in the way he worked. He would hit her in places where the bruising didn't show. He would only be abusive person to person, face to face, never via message where he left evidence of his abuse behind. He gave her a choice at times – "Either I hit Tommy, or I hit you." What mother would do anything other than take the beating herself? She couldn't imagine for a second letting Tommy take the abuse on her behalf.

And when she went to the police, he turned from an abusive psychopath to the calmest and kindest man in the world. The police couldn't believe, didn't believe that this gentle man was capable of any of the accusations she levelled at him. Patty wasn't even taken to the police station; his disguise was that good.

She didn't dare speak to Augustine about it. The embarrassment of accusing a man that the whole family thought was kind and gentle was far too much for her to bear. So, she kept it a secret from her loved ones, ended up keeping it a secret from everyone because she didn't get the help she cried out for.

She was determined that whoever killed her friend Maria and now Carmen's husband Alberto would face the kind of justice that Patty evaded all those years. She looked again at the text, piecing together the small parts into one large whole. It sickened her. She got up from the sofa, disturbing Tommy as he nodded off and ran to the downstairs toilet, by the front door. She retched, nothing to come up. As she reappeared from the toilet, Augustine walked in through the front door.

"Cuppa?" he asked, sensing a deep unease in his sister. She followed him into the kitchen without a word. The kettle clicked on, he turned around and faced her. She thrust her phone into his hand. He held it to his face and read.

"I KNOW WHERE YOU LIVE. AND I'M COMING AFTER YOU. THERE WILL BE NOTHING TO SAVE YOU THIS TIME. I WILL KILL YOU. YOU WILL DIE AT MY HANDS. AND YOUR METHOD OF DEATH? I WILL PIERCE YOUR EAR WITH A NAIL FILE."

Augustine shuddered.

35

"What have we got so far?" Augustine asked. The kids were playing on the beach. The adults had an ice cream each and sat on the wall facing their children. Tommy and Tiana were flying up the climbing frame and down the slide. Carmen hadn't been in touch since her release from the police station – and wasn't answering calls or responding to messages. Nightingale was more content watching the others and throwing the occasional handful of sand back to the ground.

"There are six potential suspects as far as we know. The two people on the top of the cliffs and the four from Girls On Tour," Angelica responded. Christine nodded.

"Not to split hairs, but that's five suspects. The two at the top of the cliff would be one suspect, as they were working together. That's the assumption anyway," Augustine explained police procedure.

"I can't stop thinking about those two. Why would they flag us down if they were the killers?" Christine asked.

"But why would they drive off before the police arrived if they were totally innocent?" Angelica asked in return.

"They may have been guilty of something – just not the killing of Maria," Augustine added, seeing the case through his detective brain rather than as an outsider. It was an important distinction. The couple could have fled because they were wanted for something completely unrelated to Maria's demise.

"So, if we discount them, that leaves four," Christine continued. "You know them better than anyone else. What do you think, Angelica?"

"Andrea doesn't seem the type," Angelica responded.

"But Gerard could be. He's got a whole lot to gain now Maria is off the scene," Augustine spoke.

"But only if the DNA test shows he's the father," Angelica responded. "Briana's business dealings with Maria could be a reason to kill. People don't like it when they lose money. And if you get caught up in dodgy deals with dodgy people, you run the risk of coming to a dodgy end."

"But doesn't that lead away from Briana rather than towards her? She's lost money in a deal, probably linked to Maria, but won't the dodgy people be the ones killing Maria – not her friend?" Augustine asked.

"And that could lead us back to the people on the cliff," Christine spoke, adding to the confusion.

"So, we look at Delia. She's been involved in business deals with Maria and Briana in the past. If we believe what we're told, then Marcus' injury might not have been an accident. So, does that point the finger at Delia?" Angelica asked.

"Hurting someone's kid is a low blow," Christine uttered, looking at Nightingale, wondering if she might ever become part of a sick campaign against Augustine at some stage in the future. She sick-burped at the prospect and swallowed the acidic contents of her mouth.

"Lower than killing someone?" Augustine asked.

"In many ways, yes," Christine responded. They all knew

what she meant. They were all parents.

"And that leads us to Carmen. The post-mortem report states that the killer might have marks on their body from the struggle. And Carmen definitely has those. Maria had her ear punctured by a nail file; the same weapon used to kill Alberto. And now she's disappeared. Doesn't look good on her part, that's for sure," Augustine mused. The two women were looking out to sea. Christine was wondering where Carmen was now. Angelica was wondering how long Maria was out there before she was spotted.

"We can't rule her out, that's for sure," Angelica replied in non-committal tones that echoed Augustine's initial doubt about Carmen.

"So, who hasn't suffered during this case?" Augustine asked, trying to pull everything into one place. The other two stared blankly at him.

"Right, put it another way. Who has suffered during these series of events? The ones that we're linking together," he asked again. This time the light bulbs went on.

"Maria is dead," Angelica said.

"Briana's son is hurt," Christine added.

"Carmen's husband is dead," Angelica added further.

"So, we have the people on the cliff, Delia and then Andrea and Gerard that haven't lost anything or anyone. They haven't lost – what have they got to gain?"

"Gerard potentially has a son to gain. Not sure what's in it for Delia with Maria's death. We don't even know who the other two are," Angelica responded.

It was the last word for some time. They took the kids home, the parents in silence, Nightingale in Augustine's arms, almost asleep. The only sound around them was the constant chattering between Tommy and Tiana. Tiana sure had a good time. But when would her mother turn up again?

Then Augustine uttered, "Maybe we need to find out what Delia has to gain."

36

"It gets like this sometimes," Angelica explained as they all looked out of the window at the incessant rain.

It started at the top of the hills. The rain ran down the gulleys made at the side of the road, splashing over every now and again as more rainwater joined at each junction. These rivers of collected rainwater all gushed in the direction of the coast.

People walked their dogs – dogs always needed walking – while wearing colourful raincoats and equally vibrant wellington boots. It was to ensure that they were seen in the torrential rain by cars whose drivers had more pressing matters in front of their eyes. And, anyway, Spain is a colourful country.

The rain didn't come often. But when it arrived it was always a deluge rather than a shower. Underground car parks flooded, people barricaded, and sandbags were deployed. Anywhere within a hundred yards of a water source was put on red alert. It wasn't just the rain that was falling from the sky that you needed to be aware of. It was the thousands of gallons steaming down the mountainsides to the sea.

Everything ended up in the sea.

37

Angelica waved goodbye to Tommy and Tiana. She had arranged a coffee date with Delia. It was something they did every now and again, maybe two or three times a year. The location that Delia had suggested they meet worried Angelica for three reasons. Firstly, they always met at the same place – Café Mira Luna. Secondly, the Javea Bowls Club was some way up the mountain on the rainiest day the place had seen for eight months. And the third reason was that she was sure the place was closed. Putting these concerns to one side in pursuit of Delia's motive to kill Maria, Angelica set off.

The one thing that Augustine said to her before she left was, "Silence is golden. If you leave silence, then the other person feels the need to fill this silence. That's when you learn the most." She tucked this nugget away at the back of her brain and set off.

Her car lurched into gear. She immediately worried that there was a problem with it. But it came back to life. Angelica looked in the rear-view mirror and noticed that she had pulled through a sizeable puddle and put the car's sluggish performance down to that.

The drive was almost completely without traffic. Not many people had ventured out into the downpour. They knew it wouldn't last. A few hours, a day at the most. And then they could go about their business again in the dry.

She raced through the streets, already a few minutes behind schedule. The trip to Javea Bowls Club was a familiar one for Angelica. Tommy's football team was run by the guy who owned it. They had their training sessions in the car park there when the weather was good enough. And all of the socials for the team were held there too.

As she headed up the hills in the opposite direction to the rainwater, the car made a juddering motion, a squeak came from under the bonnet, and it lurched to a halt. She pushed the button to turn the hazard lights on and rolled the car to the side of the road, but not too near the gulley that was reaching maximum capacity.

"What now, Angelica?" she asked herself. She knew it was a long walk back home, and quite a trek in the rain to the Bowls Club. She sat in the driver's seat trying to make her mind up what to do. Wouldn't an Uber be the best way to get to either her destination or her starting point?

She closed her eyes and waited for the solution to come to her. A knock on the door brought her back to the situation in hand.

"Car trouble?" the man said, his bright yellow raincoat standing out against everything else she could see. She said nothing.

"Problemas con su coche?" He asked the same question in Spanish.

"It just stopped moving," she replied.

"Pop the bonnet and I'll take a look if you like. I'm retired now but I was a mechanic for many years. Cars have changed so much since I stopped working on them but if it's something simple, I'll be able to spot it."

She did as she was told. He was an old man outside the car, and she was inside with the doors locked. What harm could possibly come to her?

"It's the oil nuts. Someone has loosened this one… And this one… And…"

Angelica's anxiety went into overdrive. The last straw when she left England was having her car tampered with. She was on the way to see a friend with Tommy in the car, he was pre-school and on one of his days away from his nursery. She approached a roundabout, slammed on the brakes and careered straight into the car in front of her. The airbags deployed. Tommy started crying. She was terrified.

Patty admitted it to her. But he played innocent when it came to discussing it with the police. It was at that point, when she feared that he could get to her at any point in any way, that she decided to up and leave. It was only two days later Angelica was on a plane. She'd ditched her phone, closed her UK banks accounts and closed her email account. It was only a few weeks later she learned that he'd gone to prison for hitting his new partner. There was nothing that Patty could do to reach her. Or so she thought.

But, sat on that hillside halfway between her new life and the Javea Bowls Club, she feared that he had found a way to reach her again. She leaned on her steering wheel and started to cry.

38

The phone went. Angelica looked at the number through her teary eyes. She had already thanked the man for his help and told him help was on the way. That wasn't the case, but she didn't know if she could trust him. So, he had to be shooed away.

She looked again at the display and pressed the green button.

"Angelica, where are you?" the voice asked, sounding angry.

"Delia, I've got car problems. I don't think I can make it," Angelica replied.

"Where are you?"

"A couple of miles from the Bowls Club. Too far to walk."

"Are you in your car?" Delia asked.

"Yes."

"Wait there, I'll be five minutes max."

Angelica knew she wouldn't have to wait anywhere near five minutes. Delia was known for the speed of her driving. She collected speeding tickets, always flirting with a driving ban.

It was only three minutes when Angelica saw Delia's car fly around the corner towards her. She smiled at the flashy BMW convertible. No point in having one of those when the weather was this way.

She screeched to a halt and wound the window down, waving a disposable coffee cup in the direction of Angelica who smiled got out of her car and joined Delia in the flashmobile in ten seconds flat. Everything felt like it needed more speed around Delia.

"Thank you," Angelica beamed, sipping the scalding contents of the cup, recognizing only two flavours in there – coffee and milk. This was even though she knew Delia would have asked for something else to spice it up – hazelnut syrup or pumpkin spice or whatever else took her fancy. With Delia you drank what she wanted you to drink, not what you picked yourself.

"What's up with the car?" Delia asked. Angelica shrugged her shoulders.

"About time you got a new one, anyway," was Delia's answer. It was her answer to everything.

"Shall we sit here and watch the world go by?" Angelica asked.

"Let's head just around the corner and sit where we can see the Med. I don't think there's any point in being this close to the sea and not being able to see it, do you?"

"Sounds like a plan," Angelica replied.

Sat with the Mediterranean in view, they chatted about the kids, about the weather and about the school the kids were at. Anything and everything except the elephant in the room, or the car in this case. Angelica was determined not to bring it up. She wanted to hear Delia's unfettered views on the goings on of the past few days. If she brought it up, then the answer she got would be guarded. If she let it flow then it would be Delia's words, Delia's thoughts. Angelica began to believe that it wouldn't happen. But then it came.

"Briana has a lot to answer for," Delia uttered. Angelica knew that silence was the best option here. The less she said, the more Delia would want to fill in the gaps with information.

"I think she's connected to the death of Maria and most likely what happened to Alberto. There's a business deal that's been going down. It's huge. I can tell because of the hush-hush nature of it. Usually, Briana can't help but spill the beans. She wants every Tom, Dick and Harry to know that she's found another amazing business deal. But this one isn't the same. It's going to be massive. And some people think they're going to make huge sums of money out of it. This deal is the talk of the rich and beautiful in Javea. But nobody's giving away any details."

"I can imagine how frustrating that is to you," Angelica responded, chastising herself for opening her mouth. So much for using silence as an interrogation tool. She needed more practice at this. She sipped her coffee, noticing the vanilla flavour now that it had all cooled down. Good choice.

By this time Delia had finished her coffee and started the car up, the air conditioning making short work of the condensation that had covered the inside of the vehicle.

"I have a few details. I know it's a property deal, just from the people who are involved. They're property people. And I know it involves knocking something down to build something new. That's what my ex-husband is involved in. He's the demolition guy in town. Shall we go?" Delia explained.

Angelica nodded. They chatted more on the journey back towards Javea.

"So, you want to be part of this deal?" Angelica asked.

"No, couldn't care less," Delia lied. She wanted to know what was going on every step of the way. She didn't just want to invest, she wanted to drive it. That was her way. The ice queen that she was wouldn't let on. But deep down, she wanted to know everyone's business.

As they closed in towards the centre, the conversation slowed. The roads flattened out as they got closer to the sea. The residences were more prominent and the people more plentiful. The worst of the rain was over. It was now scattered drops on the windscreen. The blue was trying to peek out from behind the greyness of the clouds.

"Shall I drop you off back at home?" Delia asked.

"Do you know what? Just drop me in the port," Angelica replied.

Angelica didn't like this creep. But he had to be in on the deal. And he'd made it clear in the past that he always had time for her. Angelica worried what he wanted to do with that time.

Laredo Paredes was a dual-purpose fixer for those in Javea who liked to operate on the wrong side of the law, or as close to it as they could without detection. He was not only a lawyer, but an accountant too. How he came about those twin qualifications was a matter clouded by years of dodgy deals. Nobody could quite make out the smoke-stained certificates that sat high up on the wall above his head. They could have been from any university in the world or none.

She had come across him when she rented her home. When she arrived in Javea, she wanted to rent somewhere as 'off the record' as she possibly could. Running away from a psychopathic ex meant that she wanted her tracks covered. Renting a place without having her name on the deeds was possible – but meant she was dealing with landlords who didn't always play by the rules. That was a risk she was willing to take.

As she made discreet enquiries, there was one common factor in all of the landlords – Laredo Paredes. He was in his thirties but could have been mistaken for any age from the early twenties to the late forties depending on the state he was in. Laredo fell into heavy drinking for long periods at a time before getting back on the wagon and cleaning up his act. The periods drinking usually coincided with immense pressure put on his shoulders by one of his clients – a tax raid, a police investigation or something else that accountants and solicitors should steer clear of, reputable ones at least.

He had long dark hair that was thinning to the extent you could see large expanses of scalp through it. His weight fluctuated with his drinking. Somehow, the alcohol made him put on weight. He ballooned and looked like he was about to burst. When he was in a good place, he went to the gym and toned up to the extent where his physique attracted a great deal of female attention. Just his physique though. His manner was enough of a repellent that even those who thought he was the most attractive man they had ever seen would walk away after only a few sentences from his vile mouth.

And when she went in to sign the paperwork for the apartment, Laredo made it very clear that he could ensure she never paid a penny in rent if she 'entertained' him and his brother for a few hours back at his place. There wasn't enough money in the world. But now she was going to use Laredo's prejudices against him. If there was a dodgy deal going on in town then he would have his fingerprints all over it.

"Here goes nothing," Angelica said to herself as she buzzed to be let into his office. She spied his secretary through the window. The view of her reminded Angelica to undo her top button. She adjusted in time for the secretary to press the button to unlock the door.

"Que?" the secretary asked.

"Laredo?" Angelica answered.

"No," was the stern reply.

Angelica had gone there on a whim. It wasn't a great loss. But she knew that Laredo would help her uncover what was going on with the property deal that now seemed to be inextricably linked to the death of her friend.

She turned on her heels and pressed the green button to let herself out. She looked up at the sky and smiled at the blueness that was inland, coming over to the coast. It would be a pleasant evening.

"Where are you going, my lovely?" a creepy voice came from the back of the room. She remembered it from the time she'd been in that office before.

"Aren't they song lyrics?" she asked.

"I don't go much for songs. But I knew you'd be back one day."

Angelica turned around with her eyes closed. She wondered which version of Laredo she would see when she opened them again. Would it be the fat drunk? Or the muscular man who looked decades younger? It was the fat drunk.

"Laredo, I wondered if we could have a chat," she stated with a determination that was palpable in the room. The secretary stopped whatever she was watching on the laptop screen in front of her and concentrated her attention on the drama building in front of her.

"Somewhere private?" he asked.

"We'll take a seat in your office if it's clean," Angelica retorted, looking over his shoulder. She imagined a smell in there that would take a whole hour in the shower to scrub off her skin when she got home.

"Perfect," he hissed like a snake.

"A necessary evil to help your friend," Angelica spoke to herself and followed him into the office.

She sat down on the seat that looked the closest to being clean. She was right about the smell.

"Laredo, I want to ask you a few questions."

"What's in it for me?" he asked. She might have known he'd want an angle. She wasn't willing to give him anything personally. But Angelica had a few aces up her sleeve from the events of the previous few days.

"You know the death of Maria Valverde?" she asked.

"Might have heard *something* about it," he responded. He played his cards as close to his fat, slimy chest as possible with everything.

"I'm not looking for information about that. I'm looking to *give you* information about that."

"Now, we're talking," Laredo said, licking his lips at the potential of some juicy information to add to his stash of knowledge. He never knew when he might need to rely on some juicy gossip as leverage.

"Well, there is now a property, and a business empire with nobody here in Spain to inherit it until her son comes of age. He will need someone to help look after his affairs," she dangled in front of him. She knew fine well that there was no way on earth Laredo Paredes would get this gig. If Jose needed protection financially, then the court would assign someone to him. They would be a court-appointed official who would be trustworthy and have all their business dealings monitored. Laredo Paredes was so far removed from this definition that even the hardened criminals he represented would be in front of him on the list of potential protectors. But there was nothing wrong with dangling this false temptation under his nose. His eyes widened with the thought of huge stacks of cash under his supervision and nobody but a small child to stand in his way of syphoning as much of it off as possible. Deep down he probably knew that he wouldn't get the job either, but with Euro signs in his eyes he was blinded to the reality.

"Now, that's interesting. I think I'll keep an eye on developments there. I thank you for this news. I genuinely had no idea. What can I do for you?"

"A property deal?"

"Again? I thought you had a property?"

"Not for me. I want to know about the big property deal that's been doing the rounds over the last few months. What's it all about?" Angelica asked, pushing her bosom up with her arms, which were situated across her midriff. She had already prompted Laredo about one of his passions – money. She wanted to remind him of the other – women.

"I don't suppose there's any harm in telling you now that it's all over," he hissed, clearly feeling that he was revealing something that couldn't come back and bite him on his enormous behind.

"All over?" Angelica asked.

"Well, it never even got started. And it wasn't meant to. You know the Montgo di Bongo bar on the front?"

"Yes," she replied. It was a Javea staple, a place to have a drink and a bite to eat while listening to the sea lapping up on the stony shore. Angelica recalled the sounds, smells and sights of the place.

"Well, there was a reported deal that they were going to knock the place down and turn the space into apartments. You know, high rise, luxury penthouses on the top, highest end of the high end and lots of cash splashing around. Only one problem…" he uttered with a smirk that told he had knowledge that protected him from the scam that he was about to reveal.

"What was that?"

"Well, you can't build that high in Javea. There isn't enough corruption in the system to bypass that rule. It's been in place for many years now. It's the reason the front doesn't look like Calpe," he explained, referencing another resort along the coast that had allowed unfettered building and subsequently looked like a mini-Benidorm.

"Even I know that," Angelica replied.

"Well, there were plenty of people who didn't. The word on the street was that you could invest in the biggest Javea property deal ever, no questions asked. Then people disappeared with the cash and the 'investors' ended up losing everything they threw into the hairbrained scheme."

"Thank you for the information," Angelica responded, getting up out of her seat. She was sure that her friends would have been involved in this in some way shape or form.

"Isn't it worth more than that?" he asked.

Angelica laughed and left. She had been in that room long enough. She needed that shower.

40

"Please stop," Carmen said. She had been hit more times than she dared count.

"You've already had one warning. This is your second and final warning. You know what happened to your friend Maria. Do you want that to happen to you?"

"No," Carmen whimpered. She wanted to get out of there.

41

As Angelica headed out from the solicitor slash accountant Laredo Paredes, she felt her phone buzz in her pocket. Looking at the display, she saw the name of her brother. If it was anyone else, she would have put the phone back in her pocket unanswered with the possible exception of Javi Jones. But she needed a friendly voice after the creepy voice in that office.

"Augustine?"

"Angelica. I've had a call from Javi Jones. He wants to meet us in Montgo di Bongo. I've never heard of the place. I don't know if you've heard of it?" he asked.

"Just been talking about it, actually," she responded. "Head to the seafront, turn left and walk until you see the sign. You can't miss it – on the same side of the road as the sea. I'll meet you there in about ten to fifteen minutes. It will take you five minutes at the most so give me a bit of a head start."

They met eleven minutes later, Angelica walking at high speed along the front. She had run and walked along the Avenida del Mediterraneo many times on fitness kicks. But the death of her friend had prompted this fast walk.

"Javi asked to meet here?" she asked, knowing the significance of the place in a way that Augustine didn't at that point. As they walked slowly into the venue, she filled him in. He went quiet, taking in the information and processing it. This was a major development but didn't have a direct line to Maria's death. Yet.

Javi was sat with his back to them, his distinctive muscular shape and angled head making him unmistakable from any perspective. The waves were lapping against the stones in the same way Angelica had imagined when Laredo Paredes told her about the deal. They approached and sat down without an invitation to do so.

"Hola Javi," Angelica spoke as she settled into a seat, moving the multiple cushions out of her way as she did. She remembered the seats being ultra-comfortable when you managed to get your position sorted.

"Hola," he replied, nodding at both of them in turn. Augustine responded with a nod and muttered, 'Hola,' under his breath.

"You might be wondering why I've asked you here," Javi spoke, looking over their shoulders at the sea. It was mesmerising for him, the contradiction of the monotony of the waves predictably crashing into the shore while each wave being completely different, just like snowflakes.

"Yes," the siblings responded at once. They were aware that his attention wasn't fully on them.

"I've been looking at a financial angle with the case and wanted to run a few things by you," he continued.

"Still a lonely police station?" Augustine asked. Javi nodded the affirmative.

"I'm waiting for credit card statements. They're coming through in dribs and drabs. Nothing unusual so far. But maybe the financial irregularities won't show on official records," Javi mused, the rolling r's making him sound much more Spanish than Welsh at that moment in time.

"So, what do you think?" Angelica asked and then remained silent. Augustine was impressed how quickly she latched on.

The silence lasted for fifteen seconds, which felt like fifteen minutes to Angelica. But she bit her tongue and resisted the temptation to speak. It worked. Javi looked disturbed by the lack of noise from anything other than the sea and the chinking of glasses at the bar behind them. Javi was sipping a cocktail of ingredients unknown to the siblings. They hadn't been served yet.

"I think that there's a big deal going down. You know, the kind that gets everyone talking. But nobody talks to a detective. Have you heard anything? You've got connections in the community," Javi asked Angelica.

"Urm…" Angelica responded, not knowing whether to begin or not. They had played their cards close to their chest so far. Would Augustine approve of her revealing the information about the fake deal to knock down the place they sat in?

"Have a think about it. I'm going to the loo," Javi spoke before she could make her mind up.

The barman came over and asked, in Castilian, what they wanted. Augustine looked confused at his sister. She took over.

"Tequila slammer. Dos," she said, holding up two fingers.

"I am sorry, but we don't have any tequila slammers. We can't get hold of any salt. Apparently, some stupid English woman is buying up all the salt from the supermarkets. Can I recommend a margarita?" he replied. Her Castilian was good, but she was clearly identified as English.

"Yes," she responded with a smile.

The drinks arrived at the same time as Javi Jones. He looked at their cocktails and wondered if he should get a fresh one himself before deciding better of it. He would be on duty for a while yet.

Augustine excused himself and went to the toilet. He didn't like visiting the lavatories at the same time as another man. Women went in groups, men solo – that was the rule.

While he was in there, Augustine thought about the case. There were jigsaw pieces that needed to be put together. He felt like they had all the pieces, but they were being put together in the wrong way. What do you do with a jigsaw? Start with the edges and then work your way inwards.

When he returned from the loo, Javi was gone.

"Where is he?" Augustine asked, trying to remember if they'd passed as he walked back to the seats and table.

Angelica had necked her drink and now it was her turn to visit the lavatory. She left Augustine alone with his margarita and his thoughts.

42

"What have you got for me this time?" she asked.

"Well, first, thank you for the people you sent our way last time. It's always nice to have a long line of new suckers. When you arrive in a new place you rely on the kindness of strangers, plus the stupidity of other strangers. You've been both for us," the man replied, looking at his female partner. His snake tattoo stood out from his ankle like it was a creature trying to get away from his skin. She smiled in return. Having people do all their dirty work made their life even easier. And all they had to do in return was share a small proportion of their profits.

"Not a problem. But I'll need a new place for my cut this time. I've dropped the key you gave me to the locker."

"We'll have to take some money from your cut to pay for a new place. They don't grow on trees, you know."

"I understand that," she responded.

The man and woman were ready to go back to the United Kingdom. Their phony deal had suckered in a great number of people. But those people would be burned now, not trusting a rumoured deal from an unknown source for a while. It was time to move somewhere new. But she could work with them again in the future. Her work had made them a stack of cash. She was rewarded handsomely. And she needed money.

That was the difference. He was doing this out of greed. She did it out of necessity.

He smiled at her. He always had a soft spot for people who

made him money, even more so if they were female. The only thing that had nearly gone wrong on their journey was the body floating in the sea. She was still upset at him for flagging someone down to help. It exposed them and could have ended badly.

But he was who he was. He had a human side that she would never understand.

"So, we're moving away from this area. We'll set up somewhere else. When we do that, we'll call you. How does that sound?"

"Sounds good," she responded with glee. She always loved the chance to make money, no matter who around her got hurt.

43

Angelica returned from the loo to find Augustine on his own. Had Javi been back? Or had he been someone else to just disappear?

"Where is he?" she asked.

"He popped back and then said he needed to go. You know what the Spanish police are like with alcohol. I think that's why they need a siesta."

"What did you say to him?" Angelica enquired.

"I showed him the key we found at the port. He asked if he could have it. Well, he actually demanded it. Then his eyes lit up and he shot off."

While she had been sat on the toilet, Angelica thought about the comment from the waiter that they had been unable to offer tequila slammers because 'some English woman' had bought up all of the salt. Added to the fact that Maria might have been killed by salt poisoning got her thinking – who in her friends would be classified as an 'English woman' by the supermarket staff?

And would they deliberately poison a friend with salt before tossing their body into the sea? She sat down and thought some more. Thankfully, Augustine was taking in the view of the Med. It was pretty. The seats by the edge were often already taken when she got there in the evening. But arriving at Montgo di Bongo in the early afternoon gave her the opportunity to sit in the prime seats. Everyone else was either at work, having lunch at home or preparing for a siesta. Maybe

Augustine was right – that was what Javi had gone to do.

The sea lapped up against the shore, rippling like the fizz on a freshly opened bottle of pop.

Then it hit her. She tapped away at her phone, hailing an Uber that stated it would be there in six minutes. Just enough time to get her head together. She would need it.

44

As they pulled up in the Uber, some people were getting into a car on the street a few houses down. Angelica could have sworn she recognized them, but she had bigger fish to fry.

Angelica paced up and down on the road before walking up the long drive. Augustine watched her silently process all of the information from the previous few days. This had always been one of his sister's superpowers. She would absorb information all the time. It appeared from the outside that she wasn't paying attention. But it was all going in. When she managed to process it all, she was highly perceptive. She could come to conclusions that others might not reach.

He followed her and watched as she rang the doorbell. Something told her that this was the woman. But she couldn't be sure. Some smart questions might reveal the answers. If not, she had something else up her sleeve.

She knocked at the door, a loud, booming knock that left nobody in any doubt that there was someone outside trying to get in. As she knocked, the door creaked and opened as it had been left slightly ajar.

"Is anyone in?" Angelica asked.

Briana stuck her head around the corner, shaking.

"Have they gone?" she asked in a state of apparent panic. Angelica motioned to Augustine to back off. He slid away behind her and stood with his back to the front wall of the house so he couldn't be seen from inside but was only a few paces away if needed.

"The people? Have they gone?" Briana asked, her entire body trembling. "They threatened me. I just hid and hoped they would disappear."

"Augustine, can you come here?" Angelica asked. Augustine walked into the house and saw a clearly upset Briana stood in her tracksuit looking like she needed help to move from that exact spot.

Augustine rushed over and helped her to a chair. He had seen this many times before, particularly in the early years of his time in the police. She appeared to be in a state of shock. She needed to sit down and allow the blood to return to her brain.

"Angelica, a cup of tea, plenty of milk, plenty of sugar," he ordered. Time was of the essence. Angelica headed to the kitchen. She knew where everything was in the kitchen. She had been there many times before. In fact, hers was the only home that the Girls On Tour didn't frequent. It wasn't anywhere near as ostentatious as the rest of them were used to.

While in the kitchen, Angelica decided to root through a few cupboards. She had turned up there with a suspicion that Briana was the killer. She was going to ask her questions, press her for answers and uncover the truth. But the scene that greeted her took her mind away from that. How could a cold-blooded killer be in such a state of shock?

Briana would certainly be described as an 'English woman' by a Spaniard. She certainly had the motive to kill after losing massive amounts of money on one of Maria's business deals. And maybe someone was there to visit her as part of their criminal enterprise. Whoever that was, they had put the frighteners on Briana.

Angelica looked through every cupboard in the kitchen. She was looking for salt containers. None with the exception of a single saltshaker, entwined with a pepper mill, two in bright colours, looking like they were people sharing a hug. No sign of massive quantities of salt – the amount needed to poison another human being.

The kettle finished its boil. She added the scalding water to the teabag, milk and three teaspoons of sugar, stirring vigourously to mix up the different elements into one coherent drink. Angelica had no idea why people took sugar in their hot drinks. If you don't like the taste of tea or coffee, then don't drink it was her view. But she knew that the sugar wasn't for taste. It was to help her get over the shock.

Going back into the living room, Angelica saw Augustine with his back to Briana, looking out of the window at the view. She was sat upright as though an electric shock had just gone though her system. When she saw Angelica, she slumped back into the chair.

Angelica wondered what Briana was doing. Augustine spun around and was surprised to see any movement from Briana, who he had left flat out on the sofa.

He helped to prop her up as Angelica neared with the hot drink. After making it look like something that was ready to drink, she had topped it up with a splash of cold water. Briana raised it to her lips and sucked up as much air as beverage, but it was a start. She slumped back into the chair. Augustine said,

"Let her rest."

He stepped out onto the balcony, checking his phone for the extended perils of dealing with shock. He knew enough to keep someone stable until the ambulance arrived. But then he passed them over to the medical professionals to get on with their work. He didn't know whether he needed to call for an ambulance in this situation or not. Something deep inside told him that there wasn't an urgency. But he needed more information. He stepped away from the other two.

Angelica was feeling vibes that Briana wasn't quite as in trouble as appearances suggested. The feeling you get when someone is asleep or passed out in front of you is a clear one. But this wasn't clear at all. Maybe the turmoil they had all been through over the past few days interfered with her senses.

She walked out of the front room and then the front door. She wanted to investigate a little more. Spanish bins are emptied into large bins situated on many of the main streets. But Angelica had noticed Briana had stuck with the English tradition of an outside bin. From there, the contents would be wheeled to the main bin and dealt with there.

Angelica neared the bin, looking behind her at the house. It was a grand place but was in need of a little TLC. The walls hadn't been painted for a few years and there were many broken roof tiles. The windows were blown in places, allowing condensation between the double-glazed panes of glass. Maybe Briana did have money problems.

She opened the bin and found that the top part of it was covered with newspapers. She never had Briana down as much of a reader. And there was nobody else in the house except Marcus. Brushing the newspapers aside, she saw two things that caught her eye. The first was a series of empty salt containers. The second was the box for a glass sharpening tool.

Angelica closed the lid of the bin and turned around to walk back into the house. She needed to speak to Augustine and call Javi. As soon as she had turned back in that direction, Angelica felt a blow to the side of her head. She dropped to the ground with the pain and looked up. She was looking directly at the sun but couldn't see the brightness. Stood between her and the bright yellowness of the sun was Briana.

Angelica kicked out at her shin to try to give herself a little bit of breathing space. But it was only seconds before Briana approached her again. Briana opened the lid of the bin and reached inside. Angelica feared that she had another glass weapon like the one found on the beach.

"A glass dagger?" she asked.

"No. That was for someone else. I dropped it on the beach. Shame Marcus got hurt. But at least that took the spotlight off me. Nobody would have ever thought I killed Maria after my poor son was embroiled in all of this. An accident but a happy accident after all," Briana explained, reaching out with her left hand to take what was in the right.

Angelica recognised the item. She had seen it many times before. Briana's perfect neon pink nails weren't the result of false nails but hours of manicuring. It was her set of nail files.

Briana opened the case with a gleeful smile. She had killed

two people already with these files. Now a third person had fallen into her lap.

"Why Maria?" Angelic asked. "Why Alberto?"

"I don't suppose it matters now. You'll be dead in a few seconds. And you can take my little secret with you. The doors between Angelica and her brother were shut off. There were two ways from the back of the house to the front. One was through the house. The doors had been locked to the balcony, leaving Augustine stuck out there. And the other means of access was by the side gate, which had been padlocked a few days earlier by Briana. She knew that she would be taking a trip to help the con artists, so she started to get the place ready to be vacant. There was no way Angelica's brother could help her, even if he was aware she was in peril.

"Why?"

"I need the money. It's as simple as that. Maria, Carmen and Alberto were stupid enough to get involved in the deal. And they lost huge sums of money. Eyewatering for someone like you. That's what happens with deals. Sometimes you win. Sometimes you lose. Unless you put yourself in a position like I did. I couldn't lose. There was no property deal. Just a bunch of suckers who were too greedy for their own good."

"But there must have been more people involved than just Alberto, Carmen and Maria?" Angelica asked.

"There were. But most of them just accepted their fate. Maria confronted me in the street like I was some common criminal. I couldn't have that. She hassled me everywhere –

social media, the school, parties, when I was out shopping. She had to go. Carmen would have followed her until she fell in line. All it took was me getting physical."

"It was you that hurt Carmen?"

"Yes. She was a good girl and learned when to keep her mouth shut."

"And what about Alberto?"

"He knew too much. He called me saying that he knew I killed Maria. He said that he'd tell the police unless I gave him his money back. Even if I wanted to, it wasn't my deal. I didn't have the money, just a small cut for my trouble."

"He knew?"

"Said he knew about the locker in the train station in Dénia. He's got businesses up there and said he followed me one day into the train station when I walked past. He wanted to give me a lift, save me getting the train, but saw me collect a bag of cash from the locker, put two and two together and actually got four. I couldn't allow him to undermine all the hard work I'd done. And now it's your turn," Briana said with an excitement that suggested killing wasn't just a way to protect her criminal deeds, but something she also enjoyed.

"What are you going to do? Kill me and then disappear to the Caribbean?" Angelica asked.

"I had to sell that place. Ran out of cash. Not that anything like that will ever happen again."

Briana reached into the nail file case. The happiness on her face faded to a grimace when she realised that there were no nail files left.

"Looking for these?" Angelica asked, throwing the nail files on the ground between them.

Briana dropped to her knees. Before she had the chance to pick up the nail files and use them, Angelica had kicked her in the ribs hard enough to hear a crack. Briana rolled onto her back in pain, gasping for breath. Angelica sat on top of her and dialled for Javi Jones. The detective was there twenty minutes later. He'd been to Dénia station, having recognised the key Augustine gave him.

Javi, Angelica and Augustine sat in the coffee shop sipping away at their cups.

"Looks like you'd make a great detective," Javi said to Angelica. Her response was just a smile.

"How are you getting on with the case?" Augustine asked.

"We've fingerprinted the locker in the station. It's got Briana's prints all over it. The cash we've found in the loft space in her house. Your testimony will help. And we've been able to match the nail files to the victims. I think we're most of the way down the road we need to be on," Javi explained.

"Anything else?"

"Briana has also been reported tampering with your car," Javi explained.

"I like your company Javi," Angelica stated, brushing her hand through her hair. She smiled at him. He returned the smile.

For the first time, Augustine felt comfortable with the Spanish-Welsh detective and his sister. He wasn't sure if that was because of the way Javi had come through in the case or the fact that Angelica told him it was purely platonic. Either way he was satisfied.

The family sat at the Lungo di Mare restaurant on the seafront. Augustine was allowed to choose as he was the one going back to work. And he was always going to choose Italian. He couldn't do without pizza for another day.

"I called my solicitor when I got back home today – the one in England," Angelica explained.

"And?" Augustine asked.

"He told me that Patty was still safely locked up at Her Majesty's pleasure. So, if it was him that sent those messages, he can't do anything about it."

"No luck in connecting the messages to Briana?" Christine said, watching the kids tuck into spaghetti Bolognese, slurping up the long strings of pasta.

"They haven't found any phones with her that might suggest she sent them."

"And the parcel of rotting meat?" Christine continued.

"UPS can't trace the order. It was dropped off at one of their depots and the account used to order and pay has been deleted," Angelica responded.

"So, what will you do sis?"

"Oh, I think Javi Jones has got my back," Angelica replied.

We'll next see Augustine in the thriller *FTM – Follow The Murders*. Read the start here –

1

"Look at you," he said.

All he got in reply was a grunt. The other man, the one laid on the floor in front of him, was far too badly beaten to offer anything else by way of reply. The floor around him was littered with teeth and blood – the result of that beating.

"And I suppose all your tribal tattoos mean you believe that you belong to something bigger?"

Another grunt. The tribal tattoos that he was referring to were all related to his beloved Newcastle Football Club. His arms sported the images of icons past – Jackie Milburn, Kevin Keegan, Alan Shearer. His right calf covered with the club crest; his left calf a magpie – the symbol of the club.

"Well, where are they now? Where are your fellow mags?" he asked, needing no reply.

He kicked at the man's ribs, hearing a crunching sound that could only have been a breakage. He smiled at the pain he was inflicting on the man. But the Newcastle fan who was laid motionless had gone beyond pain. He had disappeared into a place deep inside where he felt pain no more. His mind had left its body, the connection severed.

The attacker looked over his shoulder. There was nobody else in sight nor sound. He was alone to do what he wanted to this man for as long as he felt he could. The cold night air displayed in the vapourised breath from the two men. He saw nothing but houses either side. Here he was, within a hundred feet of more than a hundred other souls. Yet none of them knew he was about to take a life. None of them knew he had total control of the existence of another human being.

Another kick. This time no grunt. But the attacker knew that the other man was still alive. The vapourised breath told that tale. As soon as that stopped, he knew that it was all over. Until that time, he felt that his mission was to persuade the man on the ground that he had made the wrong choice in life. Persuasion by overwhelming aggression. Something like the words, "peace through superior firepower," he had heard on a television show once. He had always liked that quote.

"Well, you're now nearing the end. I think it's time to convert. Do you know the number of people who convert to religion on their deathbed? I'm told it's well in the thousands each and every year. People who have lived a life with no connection to religion, suddenly think that their soul will be saved if they believe in God for the last few moments of their life. And who knows? It might work. As for you, I'd like you to convert to a better religion. The one we call Sunderland AFC. With your last few breaths on this planet, you can save your soul by telling me the evils of supporting Newcastle and the sheer decency of supporting Sunderland."

Silence. The vapour was still there. But the man wasn't.

"Well?" he asked.

Still nothing. The man was so far inside himself that he didn't hear and didn't care. He wouldn't have the energy to reply even if he had heard or cared.

Another kick to the ribs. Another crack. Then he pulled out a knife, the blade as long as his forearm. The attacker took the knife and used the serrated edge to take the Newcastle United Football Club badge from the calf. Above it., on the man's thigh, he etched three letters – FTM.

We'll next see Angelica in *Away With The Angels*, a cozy mystery set in Javea. Read the start here –

1

"Mummy, mummy, mummy," Tommy shouted as he came out of the school gate. He was always excited to see her but this day brough particular excitement. It was the first school day of the month. And their tradition was to go and get an ice cream on the beach. The small treats went a long way with a 6-year-old boy, Angelica thought.

They walked down. She tried to walk as much as possible. In days gone by, she had a gym membership, joined exercise classes on the beach and even hired a personal trainer for a while. But Angelica found that walking as much as possible was the best way for her to keep in shape. They said ten thousand steps a day. She usually got close to double that. So, an ice cream every now and again wasn't going to cause too much of a problem.

"What did you do at school today?" Angelica asked.

Most of the time Tommy couldn't remember. When he first returned from school without memory of what had happened in the previous six hours of his day, Angelica worried. But speaking to the teacher and the other mums, she found out that this was typical. Their brains had gone from play to work. And the switch made them tired. Memories faded. As he got a little older, his memory got a little better.

"We learned about religion," he responded. Sometimes he remembered the vague topic, without much detail.

"And what did you learn about religion?" she prompted, expecting not a great deal in return.

"There are many religions in the world," he answered, sounding like a textbook rather than a child.

"And can you name any religions?" she asked.

"Catholics are one. And there is one called Islam. Buddha had a religion."

"Very good. And are you religious?" she asked.

"I don't think we've been to church, mummy."

"No, we haven't. But that doesn't mean we don't have any connection at all to right and wrong. Religion is a set of rules that define what is right and what is wrong. It is a framework to live your life by. You and I have this framework, but we don't attach it to a particular religion. Does that make sense?"

"What's a framework?" Tommy asked.

"Like a set of rules."

"That makes sense Mummy. Can I ask something?"

"Yes, of course," Angelica replied, looking down to his serious face while he walked and talked.

"Do all religions have angels?"

"I guess they all have something like angels, yes."

"And I have one more question."

"Go ahead, kidder."

"What flavour ice cream do you want?"

Angelica laughed. She wondered what went on inside Tommy's head. At least now she knew that ice ream was far up the list of things on his mind, especially on the first school day of the month.

"I think I'd like to go for a fruity one this time," she responded.

Tommy screwed his face up. "When there's all the chocolate ones, why go for fruit?" he asked with a disdain that went right through her. She knew his dislike for fruit. She didn't want it to become a dislike for people who ate fruit.

"Well, what if your mummy decides that you have to have a fruit ice cream. What would you think about that?" she asked.

He dropped his head. That was a punishment too far in his eyes.

"What are you going to choose?" she asked, already knowing the answer.

"Double chocolate!!!" he shouted back.

The pair of them sat on the wall opposite the ice cream parlour, their feet dangling over the edge, the sand below enticing them to get on with their double-scoop-in-a-tub ice creams and feel the beach between their toes.

"And did you do anything else at school today?" Angelica asked.

"I haven't finished talking about religion yet," he said

indignantly.

"Go ahead…"

"You know I sit next to Freya Gonzalez?"

"Yes," Angelica responded, picturing the young girl. The were three Freya's in his class.

"Well, she is religious. She goes to the big church in the port."

"That's a lovely church. We've been in there when we first moved here just to have a look. That's really nice for Freya."

"Freya says her mum will be an angel soon."

Angelica shook from head to toe.

"What do you mean?"

"I don't know. She just said her mum will be an angel."

Thank you for reading *The Spanish Inquisition.*

I hope you enjoyed it.

Can I ask a small favour? If you liked the book, then please post a review to spread the word. Just a couple of sentences and a minute or so of your time can go a long way. Thank you. I really appreciate your help.

If you've downloaded this book from Book Funnel then you're already enrolled in the newsletter, giving you all the information you need on Augustine Boyle and the team. It's free to join and I'll send over updates as well as some cool competitions. I won't spam you and it's easy to unsubscribe too.

Find the rest of the series at my Amazon Author page –

Amazon.co.uk: S Thomas Thompson: Books, Biography, Blogs, Audiobooks, Kindle

Augustine Boyle – The AL series

1. Off The Boyle (available free from Book Funnel)
2. INITIAL
3. PERSONAL
4. CRIMINAL
5. BRUTAL
6. DUAL
7. FINAL

The Augustine Boyle series 2 – Gary Vs the team

1. Who Killed Ellie Bright? (available free from Book Funnel)
2. Death Of A Professor
3. Murders At The F Pit
4. Death By The River Wear
5. The Threat From Within
6. The Washington Pub Killings
7. A Killer Reawakens

The Augustine Boyle Series 3

1. Marked By Murder (available free from Book Funnel)

2. Blood Luck Club

3. Mortal Coil

4. The Spanish Inquisition

5. FTM – Follow The Murders

The Angelica Boyle Series

1. Away With The Angels

Printed in Great Britain
by Amazon

75084702R00112